Pippa took a s~~ ~~ ~~ ~~the years peeli~~ ~~

Yes, she liked him~~ ~~ ~~ ~~ ~~ a different way. Fifteen years ago, her unblemished, innocent heart had believed in silver dresses and being swept away in his arms… That was all she'd dreamt of really. Perhaps a kiss…

Now, her rather bruised heart knew there was more to it.

Luke Harris was here for a month and no more. He'd made it clear that she understood they were going nowhere. He was a player, not a partner. Pippa understood his terms.

The trouble wasn't just with keeping the lion caged. Rather, it was the lioness inside her, pawing to get out…

Pippa wanted to know true passion, and she wanted to douse the torch she still carried for Luke Harris.

Dear Reader,

I have loved revisiting The Primary Hospital in London and finding out that major upgrades are underway and a new pediatric wing is near completion. It was fun meeting the current staff and patients. Pippa is a pediatric nurse and struggles to show her emotions. Luke is a visiting doctor and only back in London for a month...

At the start, it really is Pippa's story, given that Luke can't even remember when and where they first met—he just knows that he vaguely recognizes her. Gosh, that would sting!

Still, in fairness to Luke, he has very good reasons to prefer not to revisit that long ago day...

It really reminded me that we never know the effect we might have on others and that when people are going through difficult times, even the smallest kind gesture can have such an impact.

Luke might not remember, but he was incredibly kind at a time when Pippa needed that the most.

I hope you love them as much as I do.

Happy reading,

Carol xxxx

ONE MONTH TO TAME THE SURGEON

CAROL MARINELLI

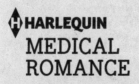

HARLEQUIN
MEDICAL
ROMANCE

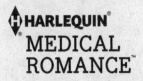

HARLEQUIN®
MEDICAL
ROMANCE™

Recycling programs
for this product may
not exist in your area.

ISBN-13: 978-1-335-59528-7

One Month to Tame the Surgeon

Copyright © 2024 by Carol Marinelli

For questions and comments about the quality of this book,
please contact us at CustomerService@Harlequin.com.

Harlequin Enterprises ULC
22 Adelaide St. West, 41st Floor
Toronto, Ontario M5H 4E3, Canada
www.Harlequin.com

Printed in U.S.A.

Carol Marinelli recently filled in a form asking for her job title. Thrilled to be able to put down her answer, she put "writer." Then it asked what Carol did for relaxation and she put down the truth— "writing." The third question asked for her hobbies. Well, not wanting to look obsessed, she crossed her fingers and answered "swimming"—but, given that the chlorine in the pool does terrible things to her highlights, I'm sure you can guess the real answer!

Books by Carol Marinelli

Harlequin Medical Romance
Paddington Children's Hospital
Their One Night Baby

The Midwife's One-Night Fling
The Nurse's Reunion Wish
Unlocking the Doctor's Secrets
The Nurse's Pregnancy Wish

Harlequin Presents
Heirs to the Romero Empire
His Innocent for One Spanish Night
Midnight Surrender to the Spaniard
Virgin's Stolen Nights with the Boss

Scandalous Sicilian Cinderellas
The Sicilian's Defiant Maid
Innocent Until His Forbidden Touch

Visit the Author Profile page
at Harlequin.com for more titles.

For Rosie,
Thank you for being a wonderful friend
Cxxxx

PROLOGUE

PIPPA WESTFORD HAD learnt to make the school library her haven.

Here she could catch up on her homework or do some uninterrupted study.

She didn't make friends easily.

Well, as a little girl she had, but her family had relocated so many times that by the age of sixteen Pippa was used to being the new girl—and always the outsider.

She had vague memories of nursery and infant school in the small village in Wales where she'd been born. Then they had moved to Cardiff, to be closer to a major hospital. As her older sister Julia's condition had deteriorated, they had moved again, to make the endless appointments in London more manageable. Then, when Julia had been placed on the transplant list, they had moved again, to ensure the tight four-hour window to get her to the hospital should a heart and lungs become available could be met.

Now, with Julia's transplanted heart failing, the library felt like her only refuge.

The chairs were heavy and comfortable, and there were lots of little nooks in which to hide. It was May—not that you could tell. The library had small, high windows that let in little light, and dark mahogany furnishings. Though the table had lamps, it felt as if it could just as well have been midwinter rather than approaching summer.

Pippa sat in a small recess, coiling her dark curls around her fingers as she read the sparse notes she'd made with the careers counsellor.

Hearing the thump of a bag, and someone taking the seat opposite her own, she took a calming breath and didn't look up. The peace she'd come here to find had been broken.

What *did* she want to do with the rest of her life?

Removing her fingers from her unruly hair, she picked up a pen, determined to tackle the blank form that had plagued her for weeks. She filled in her first name in full—Philippa—and then sighed—at only sixteen years of age she felt more than a little overwhelmed at the prospect of choosing the A level subjects that would shape her future.

The careers counsellor and her teachers had all said that the decisions she made, though important, could be changed, depending on the results of her GCSEs.

Pippa was rather certain that the results were not going to be the ones she hoped for.

She turned to the front page of her school diary and looked at the study schedule she'd meticulously mapped out when she'd started the new school year at her latest school.

Her hand tightened on the pen she was holding and she was tempted to scribble angrily all over it, or simply tear the pages out, because she'd barely managed to meet a quarter of the hours she'd allocated.

There was always something...

'Pippa, can you stop at the shops...?'

'If you can meet us at the hospital and bring in Julia's dressing gown...'

'Go and talk to your sister, Pippa. She's been home alone all day...'

Somehow she'd managed to work around all that, and then the news they'd been waiting for had come.

'There's a donor!'

Was she the worst sister in the world, because she'd sat in the waiting room with her parents as the hours had passed, wishing she'd brought her homework?

Mrs Blane would understand if her homework was late. Pippa knew that. She wouldn't be in trouble. Just permanently behind....

And now, as hope faded for her sister, Pippa felt as if her own heart was in decline. Far from being jealous of Julia, she loved her more than anyone in the world.

She wasn't just losing her sister; Pippa was losing her best friend.

'Having trouble deciding?'

Pippa looked up and blinked when she saw that it was Luke Harris sitting opposite her and, what was more, he was asking her a question.

She tried to think of something suitably witty but only said, 'A bit.'

It was hardly a dazzling response, but it was all her sixteen-year-old voice knew how to say when she was under the gaze of his brown eyes.

Everyone had a crush on Luke.

A slight exaggeration, perhaps, but certainly amongst Pippa's peers he was the most popular boy in school. Two years older than Pippa, Luke Harris was the one they all cheered on at school sports day or whispered about in assembly if he gave a speech or some such.

He was good-looking, with straight hair that was a softer shade of brown than his eyes, and he was good at everything. He had the Midas touch and, really, he was just…gorgeous.

'How did *you* decide?' she asked, both curious and wanting to prolong this small conversation.

She expected to be fobbed off, or given some vague answer, but Luke really seemed to consider her question before responding.

'I think it was decided for me, before I was born,' he said with an edge to his tone.

'You're going to be a doctor?' she asked, because she had watched the senior school's Speech Night online with Julia, and his father had presented some awards.

'A surgeon,' he corrected.

She finally looked up and saw his red eyes in the lamplight. For a stupid moment she thought that Luke—effortless Luke—had been crying, but then she realised he'd probably just come from the pool. Naturally he was good at swimming too.

Then, embarrassed to be staring, she dragged her eyes from his and saw a little graze on his strong jaw. It made her smile just a little that perfect Luke must have cut himself shaving.

He returned her smile, though his was a curious one, as if wondering what might have amused her. 'I'm Luke,' he introduced. 'Luke Harris.'

'I know,' Pippa said, smiling. 'I do pay attention in assembly. Well, sometimes…'

His smile widened and her heart seemed to do a small somersault, almost escaping the confines of her chest.

He looked at the upside-down form she had started to fill out. 'Philippa?'

'Yes, but—' She'd been about to tell him she usually went by Pippa, but then found she didn't want to get into names.

Especially if it led to surnames.

Westford wasn't a particularly unusual name, but there was just one other at their school.

Julia.

And in that moment Pippa didn't want to be recognised as Julia's sister.

They looked nothing alike—Julia was petite and blonde, with huge blue eyes, whereas Pippa was all wild, dark curls and more sturdily framed. As for her eyes… Well, last week's art homework had been to find the closest hue to your eyes on the colour chart. Try as she might to match something wonderful, like jade or malachite, Pippa's had discovered that her eyes were plain old army-green.

And even more awkward than comparing their looks, whenever anyone found out who she was there was always an uncomfortable pause, a flicker of sympathy, a particular weighty hush or an enquiry as to how Julia was doing.

Always.

Luke was in the same form as Julia, and even if she had been too unwell to attend much school this year, he'd know her.

He would also know, as everyone did, that Julia had cystic fibrosis and that her heart and lung transplant hadn't been the success everybody had hoped for, and he would naturally enquire how she was…

Pippa knew she was the lucky one.

Sometimes, though, all she felt was invisible.

The one who could take care of herself. The one whose problems really didn't matter.

What was a pair of broken glasses when your sister had been admitted to hospital that very day? What was getting your first period when your sister had just been given the news that she'd been placed on the transplant list? And why on earth would you cry over a few spots, even a face full of them, when your sister was dying?

Pippa had felt guilty, rubbing in the cream she'd bought to try and get rid of the spots. She'd clearly used far too much cream, because the peroxide had turned the long strings of brown curls on her forehead into an odd shade of orange.

Though she didn't want to admit to being Julia's little sister, Pippa loved her very much, and was terrified at the thought of a world without her. But Pippa had no one to go to with her fears, because her parents were consumed by enough fears for all of them.

It was nice, for a moment, to sit in the quiet library and talk about herself.

'The careers guidance wasn't much help,' Pippa admitted.

She had tried to discuss it with Julia, who had been happy to do so, but her mother had ushered her away and then scolded her in the kitchen.

'Have some tact, Pippa,' she'd told her, reminding her that Julia didn't have the luxury of planning a future.

And so another topic had been added to the forbidden conversation list. She certainly hadn't felt able to ask her parents about subject selection, and the fifteen-minute interview with the careers counsellor had been confusing rather than enlightening.

'What GCSEs are you taking?' Luke asked, and Pippa told him.

'I like French,' she said. 'But I don't think I could make a career out of it.'

'So you're not looking to be a translator?'

'Gosh, no. I think I'll just save it for holidays.' Pippa smiled. 'It's the same with art,' she admitted. 'I like sketching and ceramics—' she chewed on her pen for a moment '—actually, I love art. Well, I did until last week...' She suddenly smiled.

'What's so funny?'

'Nothing. Just...'

'Just what?'

He persisted, and it felt new and unfamiliar to have someone persist, to have someone other than her sister truly wanting to know her thoughts, or wanting to know the reason a smile had flickered across her face.

It was so pleasing that Pippa readily told him about the homework assignment, and the rather disappointing conclusion that the colour of her eyes was army-green.

'It's not very exciting.'

'Better than brown,' he said. 'You clearly enjoy art.'

'I do, but…' She shrugged tightly in a manner that usually would have closed a conversation, and yet he waited…waited for her to elaborate. 'It's the same as French, though: I can't see myself making a career out of it…'

'You could always combine the two and be a pavement artist in Paris…'

Pippa laughed at the very notion. 'I think I'd feel ripped off if I was in Paris getting my portrait done and I got me as the artist.' She realised that probably didn't make sense, and began to explain better, but he just smiled.

'Anything?' he asked. 'If you could be any-thing?'

She turned the question to him, 'What would you be?'

His head moved to one side, as if he'd never ac-tually considered it.

'Anything?' she insisted.

'Rock star,' he grinned.

'Guitar?'

'Oh, no.' He shook his head. 'Drums.'

'Drummers are the wild ones,' Pippa mused. 'Can you play the drums?'

'I've never tried,' he admitted, and Pippa started to laugh.

'Shh!' they were told by the librarian.

Luke came around the table and sat beside her. She could feel him next to her, reading through the notes she'd made during the career counsellor's session.

'The police?'

'Detective.' Pippa pointed to the clarification. 'That was her suggestion,' Pippa said. 'I stay calm in a crisis and I'm big on trust.' She shook her head. 'I don't think it's me, though...'

He looked at her for a long moment. 'No,' he agreed.

'You have to be in uniform first, and I can't run.'

'You can't run?'

Pippa shook her head.

'Can't or won't?' he asked.

'Both,' Pippa admitted, and then watched as he went back to the odd little notes she'd written.

'Cake?' He frowned at the single word. 'Are you into baking?'

'No.' Pippa shook her head. 'It was just... I was explaining to the careers counsellor that I'd thought about nursing.'

'But what does that have to do with cake?'

'I just…' Her voice trailed off.

Pippa knew she couldn't tell him without sounding a little selfish. She hadn't considered nursing for altruistic reasons; it was actually because of something nice that had happened. On the day she had been turning seven she had woken up excited, yet when she'd gone downstairs it had been a neighbour in the kitchen who had explained that Julia had been taken ill in the early hours.

That evening Pippa had been taken to see her sister, who by then had thankfully stabilised. Pippa had hugged her, just wanting to climb in bed beside her, but it had been all masks and gowns for adults, and she'd been told to stay well back.

Pippa had felt guilty for her own disappointment that nobody had even wished her a happy birthday, but then a nurse had come into the side ward, carrying a cake. Everybody had sung 'Happy Birthday' and for a short while she had felt remembered.

'Why does nursing appeal?' Luke persisted, dragging her back to the present.

Pippa realised then that it wasn't just his dark good looks that made him popular—he listened, and he engaged with people—with *her*—fully.

'I just think it's something…' Pippa didn't really know how to elaborate—and not just because she didn't want to mention Julia. That nurse had made such a difference. Had made her feel like an important part of the family, even if just for a little while. 'Something I might like…'

'So what do you need for that?'

'Two or three A levels, one in science. I know I want to do biology and English…' Pippa spoke in a low whisper and thought how nice it was to actually talk it through with someone. 'I really want to do art, but…' She shrugged.

'But…?'

'I don't think I'm *that* good.'

'My mother paints. She's dreadful at it…' His voice faded, as if he was lost in thought for a moment, but then he quickly regrouped, and his gorgeous brown eyes were back on Pippa. 'You really enjoy it?'

'Very much,' she admitted. She'd been taught to hold in her emotions, or to handle them herself, but in art class she felt she could let them slip out. 'I find it peaceful. Ceramics especially…'

'Then do it.'

Their heads moved closer together and she expected to smell chlorine, given that he'd just been at the pool. Or rather, given that his red eyes had made her assume he'd been swimming.

She looked up and in the lamplight saw again his reddened, slightly swollen eyes. She swallowed.

He had been crying.

Was it possible that Luke Harris was also hiding from the world in the library?

Just as she didn't want to reveal her surname, Pippa knew he wouldn't want her to probe.

Still, she did enquire a little with her eyes.

There was just a moment when each stared at the

other, and Pippa forgot about the tape on her glasses and that her fringe was streaked with orange.

It was as if both knew that behind the smiles and easy chatter there was hurt.

'Don't give up art if you enjoy it,' he said, still staring at her.

'It might be a waste. Maybe I should just focus on two...'

'But it's your favourite subject.'

'Yes.' She nodded. 'It's really relaxing. It's not like being in a class.'

'Then don't let it go.'

Pippa knew he was right—knew he was confirming what she'd wanted to hear, that she should do a subject she enjoyed—and so she nodded. 'I think I will do it.'

'Good.'

But now her dilemma was a little more solved, Pippa found that she didn't want to leave the path of his gaze. His eyes were more than chocolate-brown. She wanted to go back to her colour charts and try to identify it. Yet, despite their beauty, she could not ignore the redness of the whites and the slight puffiness of his heavy lids.

'Are you okay?' she asked.

He didn't answer straight away. Nor did he query why she might ask such a thing.

People were packing up, the end of lunch bell was ringing, and activity was all around. Yet for a moment they remained there, her question still hanging in the air between them.

'I will be,' he finally said, and then gave her a sort of downturned smile.

'Can I help?' Pippa asked, and then blushed. Because as if she could offer Luke Harris advice on anything! 'I just—'

'I'll be fine.' He stood up. 'Better get back. What have you got now?'

'Double art,' Pippa said, and his smile turned a little upwards. 'You?' she asked as they walked out of the library together.

'Double sport.'

Her art class flew by, as it always did, and as well as glazing a pot she'd made Pippa worked on a little ceramic heart to go into the kiln.

'Is that for Julia?' the art teacher asked, because she often made little ornaments for her sister.

Pippa didn't answer.

She walked home, stopping to pick up the new pair of glasses she had ordered, and also to get some groceries her mother had asked her to fetch. And then she went on to the chemist to pick up the special lotion Julia needed for her skin, now that she was spending most of her time in bed.

All the while, though, Pippa was replaying her time in the library with Luke, and then, as she turned into her street, she found herself in a daydream. One where the bell hadn't gone and she and Luke had been locked in the library for hours, days... A convenient siege situation or a blackout or something. And, given it was *her* daydream, she'd been a year or two older, and not wearing taped-up glasses with flares of orange in her hair. But what about the loo…? There were none in the library!

That tripped up her fantasy, but she decided to ignore that issue for the moment. She returned to her daydream.

When she got home, Pippa thought, Julia could give her the inside gossip on him. Perhaps she could work Luke into the conversation and find out more about him? Or even tell Julia that the totally normal crush she'd had on Luke had been massively upgraded to full-blown infatuation…

She took a breath before she turned the key in the front door. It was something she'd only recently become aware of: a certain nervousness as to what she might come home to.

'Hi?' she called out, and then saw her mum coming out of the kitchen. 'I got the shopping.'

'How was school?'

'Good. We had to think about A-level subject selection—'

'That's nice.'

'I'm thinking about—'

'Julia's got something exciting to tell you,' her mother interrupted, without waiting to hear any more about Pippa's day. 'It's good news!' She prompted an appropriate response as Pippa put down the groceries. 'But I'll let her tell you herself.'

'Sure,' Pippa said, and then headed up the stairs.

'Hey…' Pippa knocked on the open bedroom door and smiled at her sister, who was sitting propped up in bed and just finishing a nebuliser. Pippa took the mask, and was hanging it up when Julia's breathy voice came.

'Guess what?'

'What?' Pippa asked, and sat on her sister's bed.

'Luke called. He's *finally* asked me out.' Julia smiled. 'Luke Harris!'

It was selfish, Pippa was sure, to have such a painful sinking feeling…to be jealous of her sister's happiness when she had so little in her life.

'We're going to the school dance,' Julia elaborated and lay back on the pillow, her cornflower-blue eyes shining and a smile on her dusky lips.

'He just called,' their mum said, coming into the bedroom, all smiles. 'Said that he'd missed seeing Julia at school.'

'Oh.'

For a few seconds it was all Pippa could manage. She'd known, deep down, that he'd just been being nice this lunchtime and had *never* been going to ask her out. But it was such a painfully abrupt end to her daydream, to her little escape.

She forced out a more suitable response. 'That's brilliant.'

Luke came to the house a couple of times, although Pippa stayed in her room. But at school Luke looked straight through her the one time she passed him in the hall. She consoled herself with the likelihood that he was either going in or coming out of an exam.

On the night of the school dance she helped Julia with her make-up, and thought her big sister looked gorgeous in her pale silver dress.

'You look beautiful,' Pippa said as she added a little more blusher. 'Are you excited?'

'Nervous,' Julia admitted. 'But excited too!'

It had taken weeks to get Julia well enough to attend the dance. Her medications had had to be tailored for this one precious night, and there was oxygen set up in a private room at the hall should she need it. But for now she looked simply perfect.

'He's here!' Their mum came in. 'Dad will carry you down the stairs,' she asserted, 'so you can save your breath for dancing.'

'I don't want Luke to see me being carried,' Julia warned.

It was Julia's night, so Pippa stayed upstairs as her sister was carried down. She knelt on the bed, fiddling with the little ceramic heart she'd made on that special day, now on the window ledge. Since then it had been fired, and she'd painted it the closest shade she could find to match Luke's eyes. The next week she'd glazed it and it had been fired again.

Now she watched Luke walk Julia to the waiting car and felt guilty for wishing that she was the girl on his arm.

For the first time ever, she wished that she was Julia.

CHAPTER ONE

'Wow!'

On a cold November morning, when she should be dashing to get to hand-over, Pippa stood at the hospital entrance, take-away coffee in hand and mouth agape...

'It looks like a space ship.'

May, the emergency department's nurse manager, had been walking ahead of Pippa, but she too had stopped to take in the new paediatric wing at London's Primary Hospital.

For the past couple of years the east wing of the post-war concrete building had been undergoing a facelift and extension, and now the scaffolding had been removed, revealing gleaming white arches and an awful lot of glass.

'I'm getting dizzy just looking at it,' May said in her strong Irish brogue. 'I can't imagine walking along those corridors.'

'I can,' Pippa said with a smile. As a paediatric nurse at The Primary, she was thrilled at the long overdue upgrade. 'Where's Paediatric Emergency?' Pippa asked, and May let out a hmmph.

'It's the same old Emergency,' May said, rolling her eyes, 'just a fancy new entrance and a few more bays. Basically, we'll be filling up that whole place with barely any extra staff...'

'Surely not?' Pippa said, laughing.

'Well, a few extra,' May conceded. 'What's happening with your ward?'

'We'll be moving to the first floor of the new building, taking acute admissions only…'

'It won't be the same.' May voiced Pippa's thoughts. 'Anything half interesting will be admitted to its own specialised unit.'

May was right.

At the moment, the paediatric ward took everyone from babies right up till fifteen- or sixteen-year-olds, and there was an eclectic mix of patients, from planned admissions to emergencies and anything in between.

Once the new wing opened they'd be more of a short-stay ward, or a holding area before the patient was moved to a more specialised unit.

'Look at the time,' May said, flustered. 'We're both going to be late…'

Perhaps so, but before she entered the old building Pippa took one more look. She had pored over the plans that had been posted, and read all the notes about the new units, and there was one that had captured Pippa's interest.

She hadn't told a soul, but next week Pippa had an interview.

Times were changing…

And so was Pippa.

'Sorry!'

The apology wasn't aimed at him.

As Luke Harris stepped out of a side ward, a

blur of dark curls and a grey coat was dashing past, trailing a scarf, apologising to the staff waiting to hand over.

She brought the chilly autumn air in with her, but there was the scent of summer too. Perhaps it was her perfume—or was there just something about her that drew the eye?

'I'll just get changed!' she called to the gathered nursing team, and he turned his head and watched as she ducked into what was presumably the changing room.

Yes, there was something about her that drew his eye—something familiar.

Given that he'd spent the last two years in Philadelphia, Luke was more used to unfamiliar faces. Of course on his travels he'd crossed paths with the occasional former colleague, and even the occasional ex... Now that he was temporarily back in London, he expected a lot more of the same.

He couldn't quite place her, though.

There was something about the loosely coiled dark curls that made him lose the thread of his conversation with Nola, the ward's unit manager, as she took him and his junior doctor for a brief ward round, while also showing him the layout of the paediatric unit.

'As well as the cots and isolation rooms, we've twelve general beds and eight high-dependency beds, both medical and surgical.' Nola gestured to the two glass-framed four-bedded wards that were closest to the nurses' station. 'The new wing opens soon, but for now your paediatric surgical patients—'

Then she laughed.

Not Nola.

Nor Fiona, the rather eager junior doctor who had been a third-year med student at St Bede's when he'd last seen her—and an annoying one at that.

No, the sound of laughter came from the nurses' station, and Luke knew—simply knew—that it came from *her*.

Her?

Luke glanced over. Despite his rather wild reputation with women, he did at least remember all his exes, and she was not one of them. Her dark hair fell in long coils, which she was tying up as she chatted and laughed. She had taken off her coat and scarf and she stood there, solidly built, yet curvy, in pale blue scrubs. Luke was absolutely certain that he knew her.

Perhaps she'd worked at his old hospital? He'd known most of the staff there.

Indeed, that had been part of the problem. In the end, he'd felt he had no choice but to leave.

It must be from there that he knew her, Luke decided.

And if that was the case, he certainly wouldn't be acknowledging the connection.

Luke let his mental search go as they made their way down the ward and he met the patients and parents.

'Chloe James, seven years old,' Nola informed

him. 'Fell five metres from playground apparatus on Friday and suffered a lac liver. No surgery...'

Luke listened as he read through the notes and then introduced himself to the anxious mother.

'A locum?' Mrs James frowned. 'So you're just standing in? How long have you worked here for?'

'I'm just starting today—' Luke began to explain, but his attempts to reassure the anxious mother were hastily interrupted by Nola.

'Mr Harris was a surgical consultant at St Bede's, so we're very lucky to have him at The Primary.'

Luke felt his lips tighten a touch—not just at the interruption, but because the Unit Manager clearly knew his work history.

Then he glanced over to the junior doctor, and as he met her eyes he saw her go a little pink.

Ah, so Fiona must have told Nola where he'd worked. He wondered what else Fiona might have revealed...

'Mrs James.' Luke addressed the concerned mother. 'I'm sure you've seen more medical staff than you can keep track of, but I'm currently standing in for Mr Eames while he's on extended leave. I'm a general surgeon, with a specialist interest in trauma, and I'll be overseeing Chloe's care from here on.'

'So you're not just here for today?'

'No, I'm here for a month—and, judging by the look of things, Chloe will be long since home by then. How has she been?'

'Better,' Mrs James said. 'Well, she's starting to

say she's hungry, and she's asking to play games on my phone.'

'I see that,' Luke said. 'Can I take a look at you, Chloe?'

'Am I allowed to have breakfast?' Chloe asked, lifting her blonde head from the game she was playing.

'I think it's a little too soon for that,' Luke admitted, 'but I'll know more when I've had a look at your abdomen—your tummy,' he corrected himself.

'I do know what an abdomen is,' Chloe said, putting down the phone and lying back. She gave him a smile that displayed a lot of missing teeth.

'Well, I'm sorry for talking down to you,' Luke said as he lifted her gown. 'I take care of adults too,' he told her as he felt her abdomen. 'Some of them say stomach…some say belly—'

'Or guts!' Chloe said with relish.

'Chloe!' her mother warned.

And Luke laughed at the clever, cheeky young girl, very pleased that her abdomen remained soft as she too laughed at her chosen word.

'Can you sit up for me?' he asked, giving Mrs James a little shake of his head as she went to assist. He was pleased when Chloe moved well and required only the slight support of his hand to sit up.

'She couldn't do that before,' Mrs James observed.

'I'm sure.'

Chole, having terrified everyone, was clearly a

lot better than she had been when she'd arrived in the emergency department on Friday afternoon.

'They bounce back a lot quicker than us,' he said, with raised brows. 'Emotionally too.'

'Yes.' Mrs James gave a half-laugh and held out a trembling hand. 'I'm still shaking while she's begging to have breakfast. Can she have something to eat?'

'Clear fluids only for today,' Luke said. 'We don't want to rush things. I'd like to organise another ultrasound.'

'But I'm hungry,' Chloe whined, looking up at him with a glum expression.

'So am I,' Luke responded.

The little girl smiled. 'Didn't you have breakfast?'

'I didn't.' He shook his head. 'We'll get some more pictures of your abdomen and then see how you are.'

And then *she* came in.

The mystery nurse.

'Hey, Chloe...' Her voice faded when she saw that the doctors were with them.

'Oh, sorry to interrupt,' she said quickly. 'I'll come back.'

'No problem,' Nola responded. 'We're finished here.'

He knew that voice, Luke thought as he left Chloe's room and saw the nurse replacing the IV fluids.

A memory stirred...a name, a moment in time demanding to be placed.

Still, as they left the side ward, it was the patient that was discussed.

'I'd like to be paged when she goes down to imaging. If I'm not available, David?' He glanced at his registrar, who was looking at his pager.

'I need to go down to the ED,' David said.

'Sure.'

With David out of the way, Luke addressed Nola. While the polite thing to do might have been to excuse Fiona from the conversation, there was a very good reason he did not.

'I can reassure the patients and their carers as to my qualifications myself,' he said, rather curtly.

'I just thought—' Nola swallowed and glanced at Fiona, who was positively scarlet. 'Well, Mrs James was clearly worried that it was your first day and...'

'As I said, any concerns as to my professional abilities I'll deal with myself. Please don't speak on my behalf when I'm standing right there!'

Luke knew he was being blunt, but it was essential he made his position clear on this point from the start. The cloud of scandal hanging over him when he'd left St Bede's, more than two years ago, clearly hadn't dispersed completely and he didn't want it to poison his new role here.

They took the elevator up to the adult surgical units, and he walked in silence with his junior. He silently berated himself for the way he had handled the situation, because he was in no doubt that Fiona would soon be sharing far more of his past with her colleagues than just his résumé!

Gossip spread in a hospital more rapidly than any virus.

He considered trying to address it here and now, but how?

Should he *order* Fiona not to repeat what she had seen and heard a couple of years ago? Or *ask* her, maybe?

But wouldn't that just add fuel to a fire that he had fervently hoped, after two years, had gone out?

Who was he kidding?

It wasn't just Fiona.

As they made their way to Surgical Unit One he nodded to *another* familiar face—a theatre tech he'd worked alongside at St Bede's.

'Jimmy!'

'Luke!'

Pleasantries were exchanged, and they had a brief catch-up in the highly polished corridor that ran between Theatres and Surgical Unit One, but he could see the flare of interest in his colleague's eyes.

'Back in London?' Jimmy asked.

'Yes.' Luke nodded, though he could almost hear the question that wasn't voiced—*Avoiding St Bede's?*

'I went out the other week with the old mob,' Jimmy told him. 'Well, a few have moved on, but we keep in touch. Ross is a cardiac technician now.'

'Good for him.'

'And Shona moved to the ICU.'

Just for a moment Luke felt relieved at Jimmy's casual mention of her name. Maybe the world really had moved on. But then Jimmy cleared his throat and mumbled something about needing to get on, and Fiona started checking her pager, which hadn't even gone off, and Luke could feel the sudden awkwardness caused by the mention of Shona's name.

'Good to see you,' Luke said, and knew then, for sure, that he was in for a month of hell.

His…*active* sex life and his refusal to commit had been popular topics for gossip at St Bede's. Luke had always carried his reputation well—this leopard was happy with his spots and his care factor was zero when it came to gossip. For the most part his short relationships ended amicably, because he chose his partners wisely and always spelt out from the start that things would not be progressing further than a casual liaison. He would *never* settle down—and he made sure they knew that.

A couple of years ago, though, his reputation had caught up with him. Assumptions had been made about him and Shona, a married theatre nurse at St Bede's. Rumours had started to spread—as they undoubtedly would here at The Primary.

They had, however, been completely unfounded.

But Luke, for reasons he would never reveal, had been in no position to correct them.

And it was for those same reasons that he was only in London for a month or so. He was here to sell his apartment—or at least get the ball rolling on the sale of it—and then get the hell out.

This time for good.

Pippa didn't notice the surgeons leave.

She collected the charts the junior doctor had updated and then spoke at length with Mrs James, who was upset that Chloe couldn't eat.

'Why don't you go and have some breakfast away from Chloe? When I've finished doing the drugs I'll come and have a chat with her,' Pippa suggested. 'She's a clever little thing; she needs to know why she's not allowed to eat.'

'But I don't want to scare her,' Mrs James fretted. 'I need to go home for a few hours and get some milk expressed. I can't relax enough here, and—'

'And you need to see your baby.'

'Yes, but if Chloe gets upset I won't be able to leave her.'

'I'm not going to upset her. Go home and have a shower and some breakfast,' Pippa suggested again. 'Like I said, she's a bright girl. Chloe knows you need to go home this morning.'

The little girl just didn't like the fact!

As Mrs James went to collect her wash things Jenny, one of the RNs, rolled her eyes. 'She needs to learn to say no to her. Honestly... It's "Chloe this...", "Chloe that—"'

'Chloe's got a new baby brother and she's had a nasty accident,' Pippa interrupted. 'It's no wonder she's a bit clingy and her mother's anxious. Gosh,

I pretended to break my arm when I was seven just to get my mum's attention—at least Chloe's reasons are real.'

Pippa left a grumpy Jenny and made her way to the drug room, where she started preparing the morning medications for her patients.

'There you are,' Nola said as she came in.

'Just in time,' Pippa replied with a smile. 'Can you check these with me?'

'Of course,' Nola said, but rather than get on with checking the drugs she took a moment to discuss something else. 'Pippa, you know that applications close today…?'

Pippa frowned.

'For my maternity leave position,' she prompted, patting her bump affectionately. 'You often fill in for me, yet you haven't applied…'

'No.' Pippa felt a little flustered. She'd been hoping not to say anything just yet, but now Nola had specifically commented on the fact that she hadn't applied for the role she knew now was the time to tell Nola everything. 'I've put in an expression of interest for a unit manager role when the new paediatric wing opens.'

'You didn't say.'

'Because I wasn't sure if I even stood a chance. It's a big leap. I've only been a fill-in here. It's for the PAC Unit.' There were so many new specialities coming to The Primary that she wasn't surprised when she saw Nola frown at the terminology. 'Paediatric Acute with Comorbidities.'

'So, looking after chronically ill children?'

'Yes, with an acute illness or undergoing routine procedures. It sounds like a really interesting role but, like I said, I didn't know if I had a hope when I applied. I've been invited for a preliminary interview. I was going ask if you'd mind being a referee for my application?'

'Of course,' Nola said. 'But Pippa…' She pressed her lips together for a moment in slight exasperation.

'What?'

'Why didn't you say anything before?'

'I told you. I wasn't sure if I'd even get to the interview stage.'

'We've been talking about the new paediatric wing for months. All of us have been working out what positions we want…' She looked at Pippa and gave a slight shake of her head. 'Not you, though.'

'Is that a problem?'

'Reference wise, no,' Nola said, and didn't elaborate as she was called to the phone.

Pippa was left standing, and knew she'd been told off—just a little.

She was friendly enough at work, and got on with her colleagues for the most part. She'd held several nursing positions over the years and, apart from her training, her time here at The Primary was the longest she'd spent anywhere. But because she didn't bring her private life to the break room, or the hand-over desk, she was considered a little aloof and standoffish.

It wasn't just her private life where she held back, though, Pippa acknowledged. She *hadn't* joined in with discussions about careers and promotions either. She simply wasn't used to discussing her decisions with others or debating her options. She had grown up dealing with her emotions on her own, or keeping them in check so as not to upset anyone.

Nola was right—all the staff had been excitedly discussing the options and opportunities that the new paediatric wing had created for weeks. And while Pippa had been present during a lot of those chats, she hadn't told anyone about her interest in the PAC Unit.

When Nola returned, Pippa could tell she was still a bit offended, and decided an apology was in order. 'Nola, I'm sorry I didn't say anything earlier.'

'It's fine.'

'No, I should have told you. To be honest, I'm not a hundred percent sure it's the right role for me.'

'Isn't that what colleagues are for, Pippa? And managers?' Nola sounded a bit exasperated. 'We could have spoken about it.'

That was the issue in a nutshell. Pippa wasn't sure she could explain her reasons for wanting to work with chronically ill children without getting upset and teary.

She hadn't told her colleagues about Julia.

By the time she'd finished her training, attached to another hospital, Pippa had worked out that she couldn't speak about Julia without tears coming into her eyes. Her emotions when it came to her sister had been silently forbidden as a child and as a teenager. Now, as an adult, breaking down was the one thing Pippa dreaded the most, so she avoided the topic entirely.

It was one of the reasons she was nervous at the prospect of an interview.

'You're really good with the chronic patients, Pippa. I don't doubt you'd be brilliant.' Nola gave a tight smile. 'And, had you asked, I'd have told you that.'

'Thank you.'

'Do you want to run through some interview questions with me? We can do a mock-up, if you'd like.'

'I think I'm as prepared as I'm going to be,' Pippa said. 'But thanks.'

'Well, if you change your mind…' Nola offered. 'Anyway, your lac liver is going for an ultrasound sometime today.'

'I'll put it on the board,' Pippa said, and also made a mental note.

'You can tell he came from St Bede's,' Nola added. 'He's so arrogant!'

'Who?' Pippa asked.

'The locum consultant. All I did was try to reassure a patient and he snapped at me!'

'Snapped?' Pippa checked, tapping out the bubbles from a syringe.

'Oh, yes,' Nola said, and put on a haughty tone. *"I don't appreciate you speaking for me."* I was just trying to tell Mrs James that he wasn't some guy we'd dragged off the street taking care of her daughter and that he'd once been a consultant at St Bede's.'

There wasn't any rivalry, but St Benedict's—or St Bede's as it was affectionally known— was a renowned and highly esteemed teaching hospital.

'Can you update the board when you get a minute?'

'Sure.'

'Mr Harris,' Nola told her, clarifying the new locum's name. 'Luke Harris. We've got him for a month.'

Very deliberately, Pippa didn't react. With the drugs checked, Nola signed her name and then left Pippa, and she stood alone for a moment in the small annexe.

It couldn't be the same Luke Harris, surely?

Well, of course it very well could be.

She'd known that Luke hoped to be a surgeon, and had long ago gleaned that his father was a professor of surgery at St Bede's.

But if it had been Luke on the ward then she'd have recognised him, wouldn't she? After all, there was still a picture of him on her parents' mantelpiece, standing beside Julia on the night of the school dance.

Pippa cast her mind back twenty minutes or so. She'd recognised Fiona—she'd been here for a couple of months—and David, of course, but as for the dark-haired doctor in scrubs, all she'd seen was his tall and rather broad back.

Luke Harris had been her first crush—she cast her mind back—wow, almost fourteen years ago now.

Her very guilty first crush.

Her memory didn't just take her back to the warm glow of the library…instead it shot her straight back to the pain of the past.

To a time when she'd had a sister.

And then to a time when she no longer did.

Pippa closed her eyes for a moment.

Instead of being curious, or even excited at the prosect of seeing Luke again, she felt a surge of annoyance at this intrusion in her life. The jumble of emotions from the that time had long ago been sorted and put away.

Well, not exactly *sorted*.

Luke still occasionally flitted into her mind, and she blushed at the thought…

Not that anyone needed to know that!

As far back as she could remember, Pippa had learnt to keep her feelings in check for fear of further upsetting her parents—particularly her mother. And when Julia had died, Pippa had felt as if there was no one she could share her feelings with.

She'd been to see the school counsellor but, too used to holding things inside, had been unable to open up to a stranger. Julia had been the sole person she'd been able to talk to, the one person who had understood her. And, ironically, she was the only one who would have been able to comfort her in her grief.

The very person she'd needed the most had no longer been there.

At first Pippa had buried herself in art. Later, through university and beyond, instead of working through her confusing emotions she had bundled them up and shoved them into a box labelled *Too Hard to Deal With*, and Pippa did *not* want them brought back out.

And she did not want Luke Harris here, churning up and muddying waters that had taken years to settle.

Heading to Chloe's room, Pippa couldn't help but smile when she saw the little girl, purple ear muffs on and fine blonde hair sticking up, her face pouty as she lay on the bed, looking completely fed-up.

'Hey,' Pippa said, and gestured for her to take off the ear muffs—which, with a dramatic sigh, Chloe did.

'Those babies are so noisy!' she moaned, though Pippa rather thought it might be more to do with the breakfasts being given out. 'Why can't I eat?'

'Because we don't want to do anything that might upset your tummy.'

'It's upset now because it's hungry!'

'I can hear that it is.' Pippa smiled, because it was gurgling loudly as she sat down by the little girl's bed. 'It sounds very cross.'

'Have you had breakfast?' Chloe asked, and Pippa gave a less than honest shake of her head.

'No.' Pippa chose to fib, deciding her almond

croissant on the way to work was something Chloe didn't need to know about! 'I was in a rush.'

'That doctor hasn't had breakfast either. He said I might be able to sit out of bed later, but I just want something to eat...'

She started to cry, and Pippa comforted her. Really, apart from letting her organs rest and recover, one of the reasons that Chloe was being kept on clear fluids only was in case she suddenly started bleeding and had to be rushed to Theatre. There was no need to scare the little girl with too much information but, almond croissants aside, Pippa had learnt early on in life from her sister, and then later at work, to be as honest with children as she could be.

'Do you remember on Friday how they thought you might have to have an operation?' Pippa checked, and Chloe nodded. 'Do you remember being asked when you'd last eaten?'

'No,' Chloe said, but then, as Pippa gave her some tissues, she gave a little nod and wiped her tears. 'I think so.'

'The reason they asked was because if you have to have an operation then it's better if you haven't eaten. You wouldn't want to be sick while you're asleep, would you?'

'No—but I'm getting better.'

'You are.'

'I don't need an operation now.'

'It doesn't seem so. You've been resting so well, and the drip is allowing your tummy to rest too.

We're going to get some more pictures of it today, and if you keep improving it won't be long until you're able to eat.'

Mrs James came in then, and gave Pippa a tentative smile. 'Is she still asking for food?'

'I think she understands why we can't let her eat just yet.'

'In case I'm sick,' Chloe said, a touch happier now things had been explained, and willing to negotiate with her mother. 'Can I play on your phone?'

'I've got a game you can play,' Pippa said, when she saw Mrs James' tense expression. 'Mummy needs to go home for a little while.'

'No!'

'Yes,' Pippa said in a very calm voice. 'And Mummy needs to have her phone with her so I can call her if necessary.'

'You mean, call her about me?'

'About you,' Pippa agreed.

'I don't want to be here on my own.'

'Chloe,' Mrs James said, 'George has hardly seen me since Friday.'

'He's just a baby,' Chloe dismissed. 'He doesn't know.'

'He does know,' Pippa said. 'And as well as that, Mummy needs to feed him. If she has a nice quiet morning then she can make extra milk.'

'And then come back?'

'Of course I'm coming back,' Mrs James said.

'But what if I have to get my X-rays while you're not here?'

'Then I'll come with you,' Pippa said, and looked at Mrs James' torn expression. 'Chloe, nobody's going to forget you.'

Chloe looked anxiously over to her mum. 'Promise?'

'Of course I'm not going to forget you, silly,' Mrs James said as she kissed and hugged her daughter.

There was plenty to do before Pippa got around to updating the board—erasing *Locum* and writing *Mr Harris*, while explaining to her nursing student that doctors who had completed their fellowship for the Royal College of Surgeons were to be called Mr.

'What if they're a woman?'

'Still Mr,' Pippa said, and then, seeing the student frown, she smiled. 'I was joking—they're called Miss.'

'What if they're married?' the student asked.

'Still Miss,' Pippa said, answering the questions easily and not letting anyone glimpse how unsettled she felt—a skill she had honed to perfection.

Luke Harris had been the beat of her heart for months.

No, make that years!

Even before that conversation in the library she'd had a crush on him, just as most of her friends had, but after the day in the library…after he'd arrived to take Julia to the dance… When things had got hard at home, she'd used to picture herself in a silver dress, being led to a waiting car.

She could still, with absolute clarity, remember the thrill of him speaking to her that long-ago lunchtime. Taking the time to really listen to her.

She recalled it now.

Not so much the conversation they'd shared, but how she'd felt listened to—how it had felt to be in the spotlight of another's attention, rather than constantly on the periphery…

Luke Harris had made her feel as if her thoughts, her opinions, really mattered. And even if she hadn't told him she was Julia's sister, he'd made her brave enough to share other little parts of herself.

The memory of the library made her want to cry, for some reason, and crying was something Pippa simply did not do.

Certainly not at work.

Nor with family—heaven forbid!

Not with anyone.

Not even herself.

Her last relationship had ended with a dash of bitterness.

'The thing is, Pippa, I don't know you any better than I did the first night we met.'

Another relationship fail.

Another round of being told that, despite her friendly demeanour, there was nothing behind that wall.

Because she never let anyone in.

Oh, sex was okay—ish. Though she took for ever to be seduced into bed, and then very quickly decided she ought to go home, or wished that he would…

No pillow-talk for her!

She wasn't a superficial person—in fact, her emotions ran deeper than most people's. Pippa just preferred her relationships to be that way: on the surface. She didn't know how to share her feelings, let alone her private thoughts. Just as she didn't know how to drop Julia into the conversation, and neither did she know how to tell someone she was dating that she was a carrier for CF.

At the age of twenty she'd made the decision to get tested, to find out if she was a carrier, and the counsellor at the clinic had asked if she had support…

'I do,' Pippa had replied. *'I just want to know.'*

She had the same support she'd relied on since she was a little girl: herself.

'And you understand that even if you are a carrier, it doesn't mean your child will have CF. The father would have to be a carrier too, and even then…'

She hadn't told her parents the result.

They'd never asked, but then they so rarely asked anything when it came to her.

Instead, even though she hadn't been dating anyone at the time, Pippa had gone on the Pill, and was always careful to make sure her lovers used condoms.

There had never been an accident.

Sex had never been exciting enough for breakages!

CHAPTER TWO

IT WAS A typical busy day on the paediatric ward, yet an extremely untypical one for Pippa.

She felt as if she was on heightened alert and kept glancing at the corridor, or towards the nurses' station, where doctors often gathered. It was a relief when the day neared its end—especially when Mrs James called to say she was half an hour away.

'I'm just about to take Chloe down to Imaging,' Pippa informed her. 'I'll let her know that you'll be waiting for her when she gets back to the ward.'

'The porter's here,' called Kim, the sister on late duty. 'If Mrs James isn't back in time then I'll send someone down to relieve you,' she assured her.

Escorting Chloe, Pippa was simply pleased to have made it through the day without seeing Luke. She wanted to get her head together before facing him.

Still, even if she was aching to get home and somehow process the fact that Luke was actually working here at The Primary, she kept her smile on for her patient.

'Do you remember being in here on Friday?' Pippa asked Chloe as she and the porter wheeled her to Imaging.

'Not very much,' Chloe said. 'They gave me an injection. It made me sleepy.'

Chloe had had a CT on Friday, with contrast, but today it was an ultrasound.

Just as the procedure was about to get underway, the radiologist looked up and smiled. 'Hey, Luke.'

'Mike! I didn't know you worked here.'

Pippa felt her throat go tight. Even before she glanced up, just hearing his voice confirmed her worst… Was it fears? Her worst fears? Or actually her deepest wish?

She wasn't sure. All she was sure of was that it was most definitely him.

Luke.

She glanced over and found she couldn't tear her eyes away.

Age had *not* wearied him.

Gosh, he'd been a stunning teenager, but as a thirty-something man he was far beyond stunning. That straight hair was superbly cut now, and he looked incredible in his dark navy scrubs, but she couldn't comment on his dark brown eyes because Pippa found that she dared not meet them.

He was big—or rather tall—his shoulders were broad, as if all those years of swimming had paid off, and the slender youth was now a very solid man.

'Hey.' He gave her a brief smile. 'You're from the ward?'

'Yes.' She nodded, but then abruptly looked away, as if it were her heart on the monitor, about to be examined and exposed. 'Chloe was a bit upset about coming down to Imaging without her mum.'

'You'll be fine,' Luke said to the little girl. 'It's

not going to hurt at all. It may be a little bit uncomfortable, but we just want to take a good look.'

'How was America?' Mike asked as he washed his hands.

'Incredible,' Luke said.

'You've been to America?' Chloe asked, and Pippa was very grateful for a nosy seven-year-old who could ask any question she chose to when her little tummy was about to be examined. 'Did you go to Disneyland?'

'I didn't,' Luke replied.

'Why not?' she asked, clearly appalled that he'd go all that way and not go to Disneyland.

'I was in Philadelphia. That's a long way from the theme parks.'

'But you could have gone on the way,' Chloe insisted. 'My friend Sophie went to New York, but they stopped at Los Angeles on the way.'

'Why didn't anyone tell me I could do that?' Luke said, smiling at her idea of geography.

'We're going to Disneyland Paris. Mum promised me on Friday.'

'Oh, I'll bet she did,' Luke said with a grin. 'What else did you wangle?'

Pippa found that she was smiling too, because he'd clearly worked with children before and knew their ways.

'I'm getting a new lampshade for my bedroom, and Daddy bought me these earmuffs—' she held up her bright purple fluffy present '—so I don't hear George crying all the time when I'm at home.'

'Sounds like you're being very spoilt,' Luke said, distracting Chloe as the radiologist probed her abdomen. Yet while he chatted easily his eyes were hawkish as he stared at the screen and Chloe's liver was examined, the laceration measured, and her abdomen was checked for any free fluid. He seemed pleased with the findings, and soon the sheet was back over Chloe's stomach.

'Thanks, Mike.'

He glanced over to Pippa and gave her a very brief smile—the same bland smile he had given to the radiologist—and it was clear to Pippa that he didn't remember her at all.

She had to wait thirty minutes for porter to arrive and take Chloe back up to the ward.

'Oh, sorry.' Kim glanced up when Pippa returned to the ward. 'I forgot about you. Mrs James is here.'

'It's fine,' Pippa said.

'Can you settle Chloe back into bed?' Kim asked. 'Laura's taking care of her tonight, but she's in with Cot Two. His drain is blocked again.'

'Sure.'

It was actually Mrs James who needed settling. 'Surely someone can tell me how the ultrasound went?' she said.

'The staff are a little tied up, but I'll remind them to come and talk to you.'

Pippa knew that the evening meals would soon start to be given out, and mealtimes were particularly difficult for her patient right now. She could see the very active little girl was starting to feel better and her mother was going to have her work cut out to keep her quiet and resting. 'Chloe… Do you like jigsaws?'

'No.'

'We've got some Disney ones.'

Her face lit up, and by the time Pippa had found a couple of jigsaws to keep the little girl amused she was almost an hour past the end of her shift.

Not that she minded, because when her phone buzzed, and she saw that it was her mother, she actually breathed out a sigh of relief that she was still at work.

She often dropped in on a Monday, if her shifts allowed, but today Pippa really wanted a night to herself.

'I'll come over at the weekend,' Pippa told her. 'Well, I'll try.'

'You haven't been to the cemetery for a while.'

Pippa could hear the slight accusatory tone of her mother's voice and ducked into a treatment room to continue the call.

'No,' she said. 'Work's been busy.'

She could hear her own excuses, her own lies. Her mother went to visit Julia's grave most days, but the truth was that Pippa drew no comfort from going.

'We're flat out…' she started to say, but then paused as the overhead chimes went off. They weren't for Pippa's ward, but she was thankful for them all the same.

Once she'd called her mother from home, pretending to be at work. A neighbour had knocked at the door and Pippa had felt caught in the lie. Another time, she'd been in the Tube station on her way home and an announcement had given her away. She felt guilty for not going to see her parents, but relieved at the same time—and wishing it didn't have to be this way.

This evening Pippa knew she couldn't face them. She really just needed to be on her own.

She glanced up and felt a blush spread across her cheeks as Luke came into the treatment room and started going through the drawers.

'We're really short-staffed,' Pippa said to her mother once the emergency chimes had gone quiet. 'So I'm staying back. I really do have to go. Love you…'

She let out a tense breath and then pocketed her phone, relieved that was over—at least for now. But then she looked up and saw Luke turning on the light over the treatment bed. Her sharp intake of breath was just as tight when he spoke.

'Would you be able to give me a hand?' he asked. 'I need to reposition a drain and I'm going to bring him in here.'

'Cot Two?' Pippa checked. 'I think Laura's taking care of him. I'm actually finished for the day.'

'Oh! I thought I just heard you say you were staying back…'

She gave a small laugh, albeit through gritted teeth. Weren't private conversations that you were

forced to have in a place where you could be over-
heard supposed to be politely ignored?

Not only that, but Luke persisted. 'Tut-tut,' he
said as he located the alcohol swabs and tape.

'Sorry?' Pippa did a double-take, a little unsure
as to what he was referring to.

'Pretending to be stuck at work… I find honesty
a much better policy.'

'Not when it comes to my parents.'

'Oh!' He smiled. 'My mistake.' He took a hand-
ful of saline flushes and added them to the dish
he was filling and then looked right at her. 'In that
case, I totally get it.'

It was an odd conversation, being pulled up for
a white lie and at the same time meeting his eyes
properly.

They were still the same beautiful kaleidoscope
of shades of brown. He still had the same thick,
dark lashes that barely blinked as he held her gaze.
She stood in silence, trying to decipher if the flare
of interest that had ignited between them was recognition or attraction.

Pippa knew that in her case it was both.

As for Luke, she wasn't sure.

'I'll let Laura know you need a hand.'

'No need.' He gave her a small smile that perhaps
meant he wasn't really in need of a hand after all.

He stared right at her and Pippa felt flustered.
For once, she was worried that she might actually
be showing it, because she could feel heat spread-
ing up her face.

'I'd better go,' Pippa said, although her feet refused to obey and she stood there, still facing him, trying to think of something to say. 'Oh, and Mrs James wants to know what's happening after the ultrasound.'

'Yes,' he said, his eyes never leaving her face.

It would seem that Luke Harris was either trying to place where he knew her from or blatantly flirting.

Or both!

'Do I know you?'

Pippa didn't answer. She didn't want to be evasive, but his words hurt—like a boot stomping in those muddied waters she'd fought all her life to clear, and she wasn't quite sure of the strength of her voice even if she were able to find the right words.

His eyes narrowed a little, as he obviously kept trying to place her, yet Pippa found she was looking at the dark shadow of his jaw, and the loosened tie around his neck. His jacket was off, sleeves rolled up, and his citrussy scent was somehow morning-fresh, because it cut through the antiseptic smell of the treatment room.

It was hell to know she was attracted to him all over again.

He seemed to take her silence as a game. 'I'll work it out,' he said, and then turned away and carried his tray of items over to the treatment bed, to prepare for his patient's arrival.

She felt as rattled and jolted as the Tube that took

her the couple of stops to her home, and the feeling refused to leave her as she went up the stairs to her tiny and very cold flat.

Pippa turned on the electric throw, which she carried with her between the living room and bedroom, before stripping off.

It was so nice to have a shower and pull on her dressing gown, and then, for the first time in…well, in a long time, she went to take a certain photo album from the shelf.

Pippa's mother had had every single photo of Julia printed for her, as well as other family shots and ones that the school had given them.

Her parents had an almost identical album, but unlike Pippa they went through it most days—at least most of the days that Pippa was there. It sat on the coffee table, or in the kitchen.

Pippa's album was tucked away on a low shelf, not at eye-level. Present, but not immediately visible. And even though her hand went to it straight away, as she took it from the shelf she paused, and her fingers closed over the little ceramic heart she'd made in art that long ago day.

Gosh, she'd been crazy about Luke Harris then.

Now, sitting on the sofa, with her warm blanket wrapped around her, Pippa went slowly through the album.

Julia's first, second and third birthdays. She'd looked so chunky and healthy then, but already she'd been sick.

Pippa knew that Julia had been in hospital even on the day Pippa was born.

Her mother had once proudly stated how that night she'd been wheeled from Maternity down to the children's ward, to stay with her fretful toddler. Newborn Pippa had been left alone with the other babies on the ward.

She turned the page and there was a photo of the two of them on a beach. Julia, ever the big sister, was holding Pippa's hand. Then there was the first day at infants school, junior school, new houses, another new school...

God, she missed Julia so much.

She felt so very cheated on her behalf for the life her sister had never got to live.

More than a few times her mother had shamed Pippa by accusing her of being jealous of the attention given to Julia.

Had she been?

Pippa sat quietly, finally asking herself a question she'd buried deep down inside her.

Maybe? she ventured. *Sometimes*, she admitted. Especially when she'd been a little girl.

Yet for the most part, especially as Julia's condition had deteriorated, *jealous* wasn't quite the right term to use.

Their parents had done all they could to cram so much into Julia's too-short life—trips to theme parks, swimming with dolphins and grand days out—almost willing her to live on for a few more months. And for eighteen years Julia had obliged.

Living, but slowly growing almost translucent.

After the dance, Luke had faded away too. Pippa's mum had said that Julia didn't want him to see her so weak.

So weak…but in other ways so incredibly determined and strong.

One night Pippa had padded out of bed and climbed into Julia's…

'Clever you!' Pippa had said, because Julia had found out that day that she had been accepted into the University of St Andrew in Scotland.

The prestigious university had been Julia's first choice, and despite a failing heart and lung transplant, and endless stays in hospital, as well as multiple procedures and appointments, Julia had made schoolwork her priority.

Pippa had always been in awe of her sister, and never more so than that day.

Julia must have known for some time that she hadn't a hope of going to Scotland and St Andrew's, yet she'd studied incredibly hard and had got the most amazing grades.

Pippa had known that if it had been her she'd have given up long ago, or decided there was no point, yet Julia had pushed herself, living as if she wasn't dying, grabbing on to life and making the most of every precious moment, even if it led nowhere.

'How does it feel to get in?' she'd asked her.

'I made it…' Julia had breathed.

'You did.'

'Go and see it for me.'

'You'll go yourself.'

'Stop,' Julia had said huskily. 'I do the happy-clappy routine for Mum and Dad, but I don't want to put on an act with you.'

'You don't have to.'

It was true. Though their mother had done her level best to police their conversations, they'd always found time to talk—really talk—as only siblings could.

'Will you go and see it for me?' Julia had asked.

'I don't know...'

She'd lain beside her sister, and Julia had stroked her hair. Her wonderful sister had comforted her as Pippa had let a sliver of her fears out.

'I think it would be too much. I mean, I can't imagine going anywhere without you.'

'I'm so tired, Pip.' Julia was the only one who had called her that.

'I know.'

'Tired of fighting...just to breathe. I'm ready.'

'I don't want to let you go,' Pippa had whispered.

She'd paused and taken a deep breath, because she'd known her mother would forbid this conversation if she knew.

'Are you scared?'

'No,' Julia had said, but then she'd hesitated. 'Pip, everybody gets scared at times. I just tell myself I'll let myself be scared tomorrow.'

Pippa hadn't known what she meant, but then Julia had asked, 'Are you scared?'

Pippa hadn't wanted to upset her sister, but her answer had been honest. Almost. *'Sometimes.'* The truth was that she'd been petrified. *'I don't want to be on my own.'*

'You've had a lot of time on your own,' Julia had said, wise beyond her years. *'Really, you've always been on your own.'*

'I've had you,' Pippa had stated, though she'd known Julia was referring to the disparity in the way their parents treated them. It was the first time it had properly and openly been acknowledged between the girls.

That truth had opened the door for Julia to reveal her real fear. *'I'm worried about them. How they'll be when I'm gone...'*

Pippa had wanted to reassure her sister, to tell her that things would be okay, to say she'd be there for their parents, but Pippa had been worried about that too, and had known in her heart that she wouldn't be enough to fill the gap.

She could never come close.

'They'll keep on loving you, the way they always have,' Pippa had said.

And absolutely her parents had.

At home, even now, it was almost as if Julia had never left. Her bedroom lay untouched; her clothes still hung in the wardrobe. Pippa's old bedroom, on the other hand, was now her mother's sewing room.

Fourteen years on, Pippa looked at the picture of her sister in her silver dress and ran a finger over her pretty face.

Translucent. That really was the word for Julia, because even in the photo it looked as if she was fading.

But not Luke. He stood bold and confident, wearing a suit as if he'd been doing so for a lifetime.

Even if he didn't know it, Luke had helped Pippa a lot, emboldening her to make choices she might not have otherwise. She would never regret taking art.

Returning to school after Julia had died had felt so odd. People had avoided asking her about Julia, or simply avoided her altogether. And there had been no Luke Harris to daydream about bumping into. He'd been off on his gap year. Her one solace had been the chalky, papery smell of the art room. It had become a haven from the despair of life at home.

Back then Luke Harris had still popped into her thoughts, into her daydreams and dreams. But now Luke was back in real life.

In real time.

Grown-up time.

He'd asked where he knew her from and she'd hesitated to answer. He'd taken it as a tease, but she'd actually been completely tongue-tied.

Was it ridiculous to be hurt that he couldn't place her or recall the precious hour they'd shared?

He'd forgotten.

And forgotten was how Pippa had felt all her life.

His question 'Do I know you?' had catapulted her straight back to the agonising times of her youth.

I loved you! she'd wanted to shout.

Yet that would have been her teenage self responding to him.

Teenagers knew nothing about love.

Now she turned over the little heart she had painted that day in art class. Kobicha-brown, copper and russet—all the shades of his eyes as she'd gleaned in that precious hour alone with him.

Pippa managed a little laugh at the intensity of her own teenage emotions, then tried to rationalise their long-ago conversation.

He'd simply been being nice. Doing his polite Head Boy duty and helping a younger student.

Apart from attending the same school and having one conversation in the library, they didn't share a past.

Julia was really their only connection.

That was all.

CHAPTER THREE

PIPPA WASN'T THE only one to notice Luke.

It wasn't just his effortless charisma and dark good looks that had people talking, nor his clear skill as a surgeon. It wasn't even the slightly detached arrogance that ruffled some of the staff.

Luke Harris had come to The Primary with scandal attached!

Louise on Maternity had once briefly dated him—or so one of the midwives had told Laura when she'd gone to borrow a breast pump. And on her return had gleefully spread the word.

Oh, and one of the domestics had worked in the residences at St Bede's when Luke had been a medical student there.

As for Jimmy, the theatre tech, he seemed delighted to tell tales of a decadent past.

Rumours swirled in abundance.

Now, on the eve of Pippa's interview, as she sat at the nurses' station in a brief lull as they waited for the late staff to arrive, Luke was the topic of conversation. Pippa was trying not to listen, and to focus instead on that morning's patient discharge papers. She was tempted to ask Chloe if she could borrow her earmuffs as the conversation again turned to Luke.

Jenny was feeding little Toby his bottle at the nurses' station, as his parents hadn't come in yet, as well as providing updates on the sexy new consultant. 'He was just made consultant and then suddenly he threw it all in.'

'I'd hardly call studying trauma in Philadelphia throwing things in,' Nola responded. 'With all that experience he'll be scorching hot and snapped up wherever he goes.'

'Yes, but that wasn't why he left. He was sleeping with one of the senior theatre nurses and it all blew up.'

'Who *hasn't* he slept with?' Nola sighed, and then let out a soft laugh. 'Aside from us!'

But that wasn't all the gossip Jenny had. 'She was married; her husband worked on the ortho—'

Jenny halted abruptly and, glancing up, Pippa knew why the conversation had been so rapidly terminated. The man being discussed was making his way down the corridor towards the unit.

'Sorry to interrupt,' Luke said drily, as if he knew he'd been the subject of the conversation. 'Martha wants to discuss a patient with me.'

Martha was the paediatrician.

'She's in the ED,' Nola said.

'Is Fiona here?'

'No,' Jenny said, shaking her head. 'She was a short while ago, but she got paged to go to Surg One. They sound busy.'

'Then I'm hiding here,' Luke said, and took out a wrapped canteen sandwich from his pocket.

'Why aren't you eating in the consultants' lounge?' Nola asked.

'That's a very good question,' he replied, nodding, though Pippa noticed he didn't answer it. He looked at baby Toby and said, 'Somebody's hungry.'

'You are, aren't you?' Jenny cooed to the baby.

Pippa glanced over and couldn't help but smile. Jenny might be a dreadful gossip, and to Pippa's mind somewhat abrupt with the parents, yet the babies and children adored her.

Even Toby, a little 'Failure to Thrive' and known to be a fussy feeder, was taking his bottle and gazing up at Jenny in adoration.

'Toby knows better than to not drink his bottle,' Pippa teased. 'He must know you like your charts to be neatly filled in.'

'Absolutely, I do,' Jenny agreed.

When Nola took herself off to the office, Jenny looked at Luke.

'I was in the army for ten years,' she told him.

'Paediatrics?'

'Mostly.' She nodded. 'A couple of years on Maternity in Germany.' She sat Toby up to burp him. 'You were at St Bede's, weren't you?'

But Jenny's fishing expedition ended as Toby's father arrived, and her rather brusque tone returned as she addressed him.

'I thought you were going to be here to give him lunch, so that I could observe.'

Pippa glanced up and saw Luke's subtle eyebrow-raise as Jenny headed off with the somewhat sheepish father.

'Is she always so approachable with the parents?' he asked.

Pippa didn't reply to his sarcastic question, just turned back to her work. But she could feel her neck turning pink and knew his attention was on her. In the days since their paths had first crossed she had occasionally felt his eyes on her, just as they were now. She felt his gaze rather than met it, and it was the most deliciously unsettling feeling she'd known—a flutter of nerves dancing through her veins as she quietly thrilled at his long assessment.

'I do know you,' Luke said. 'I just can't work out how.'

'Because I'm so unforgettable?' Pippa teased. Or was she flirting? Or just covering up how much his vague remembrance hurt when *she* could repeat their conversation verbatim?

'Pippa, I'm saying that I know you from some-where—not that I've slept with you. I'd certainly remember if I had.'

She actually laughed.

'So,' he persisted, 'where *do* I know you from?'

She was about to tell him, but for one teeny second she was back there, in the library, being listened to for what had felt like the first time in her life. Feeling important. Not an important person, just important enough for someone to listen to her...

'That's mean,' he said, taking her silence as refusal. 'Come on, Pip...'

'Pippa!' she warned, just as she did with anyone who called her that, because only Julia had ever called her Pip.

'Then it's lucky for me that I don't have a speech impediment.'

Pippa couldn't help her reluctant smile at his unsuitable joke as she filled in her paperwork. 'If you want to be precise, my name's actually Philippa.'

'Oh, I'd love to be precise.'

His words were delivered in a low voice, for her burning ears only. Burning because a roar of heat had moved from her throat to her scalp. It seemed he was taking their little *Where do I know you from?* game up a notch.

She should possibly warn him that he was wasting his time. Pippa was the last person to get involved with someone at work—especially some visiting locum who came with a side dish of scandal.

But this scandalous visiting locum was Luke Harris.

And for Pippa that changed everything.

Still, she was saved from responding as Jenny and Nola returned.

'Still here?' Jenny asked him in her blunt way.

'Yes,' Luke answered easily. 'I'm trying to work out where I know Pippa from.'

'Do you two know each other!' Jenny gaped.

'I'm sure we do.'

'How?'

Pippa chose to put him out of his misery. 'We went to the same school.'

'Did we?' His eyes widened as he took in the news.

'You two were at school together?' Nola was clearly delighted by this snippet of news.

'Hardly together,' Pippa said. 'He was two years above me.'

Should she remember that? Pippa pondered. If she hadn't been so crazy about him, would she recall that detail? But then she came up with a good excuse as to why she might.

'He was Head Boy in his final year.'

'Did you have a crush on him?' Nola teased, from the safety of being six months pregnant and in a happy marriage. 'I know I would have.'

Pippa casually shrugged. 'Everybody did.'

'Get out!' Luke refuted.

'Come off it,' Pippa said with a smile, stapling the discharge papers and standing up to file them. 'It's true and well you know it.'

'Were you on the swimming team?' he asked, clearly still trying to place her.

'No.' She looked over, and with her eyes willed him to remember their one conversation, that lunchtime in the library, when the world had stopped for a slice of time.

He looked at her lanyard, clearly to read her surname. The recognition obviously startled him and he looked up in shock.

'Westford... So you're Julia's sister?'

Of course that was how he would remember her. She swallowed down the hurt and nodded.

'You have a sister?' Nola asked with a hint of surprise and also some confusion. 'Julia?'

'I… Yes,' Pippa managed, unsure how to voice the fact that her sister was dead and uncertain how to handle the fact that she had never mentioned her. 'I *had* a sister,' she added, unable to say outright that Julia had died, watching Nola's smile fade as she heard Pippa place her sister in the past.

'Oh, Pippa…' Nola said as she stood. 'I had no idea.'

'It's fine.' Pippa put up her hand to stop Nola from coming over, but Nola just kept on walking towards her.

'I'm so sorry.'

'Thank you,' Pippa said automatically, feeling her nose pinch and terrified of breaking down. She got up from her seat.

Damn you, Luke, Pippa thought. *Damn you for resurrecting these feelings in me.*

She'd hoped to leave all that pain and confusion in the past. But rather than discuss the agony of loss, it felt easier to voice a different hurt, and so, as Pippa walked off, she threw over her shoulder, 'Luke used to go out with her.'

Luke was about to correct Pippa, and say that he had never gone out with her sister, but then he halted himself. Because this certainly wasn't the place. He could see that her face was on fire and knew that she was upset. It was clear her colleagues hadn't known about Julia and that he'd just revealed something she had carefully kept to herself.

Boy, he'd messed that up, Luke thought, seeing Nola and Jenny exchanging quizzical looks and then turning to him.

'Luke?' Jenny said, clearly hoping for more information.

But Luke would not be enlightening the two nurses further, nor offering any explanation. Instead, he followed Pippa down the corridor.

He had been messing about…just making light conversation, Luke told himself. His stride briefly faltered, because *of course* he'd been flirting. He'd been determined to avoid all that during his brief time here. But then attraction had flared from the moment he'd locked eyes with Pippa. Before that, in fact. For awareness had been there from the moment she'd dashed past him that first morning, her scarf trailing behind her and bringing with her the scent of summer. He'd wanted not just to remember her name and where he knew her from, but to get to know her some more.

No, it hadn't been idle conversation—and he was the one who'd brought the private game they'd been playing right up to the nurses' station…

In fact, he'd been pleased to have an excuse to take a quick break on Paeds. He'd tried to tell himself that Pippa wasn't the only reason he'd taken his lunch there. But he knew he'd been hoping to suggest meeting up away from work. And now their discreet little flirtation had got out of hand.

His eyes briefly shuttered in self-recrimination, because he'd clearly not only hurt her, but in bringing up her sister he'd been indiscreet—and that was most unlike him...

He knew from bitter experience the damage careless words could cause. Loose lips didn't just sink ships—they torpedoed relationships, changed the course of careers, capsized lives...

He thought back to his old hospital, to those last painful weeks at St Bede's and the conversations that had abruptly halted when he'd walked into the break room—people had acted the same way Jenny and Nola would undoubtedly act now, when Pippa returned to the desk...

Only on this occasion it was entirely his fault.

'Pippa,' said Luke, as he caught up with her in the kitchen. 'I'm so sorry about that.'

'About what?' Pippa asked, pouring hot water over a teabag for a drink she didn't even want—it had just been an excuse to get away.

'If I spoke out of turn about Julia.'

'You didn't.' Pippa attempted a nonchalant shrug, but her neck and shoulders were so rigid that all she did was slop her tea. 'It's not as if it's a state secret or anything,' she said, mopping up the little spill on the bench, glad to have something to focus on rather than look at him.

'It's clear they didn't know.'

'Only because it's never really come up,' Pippa responded, picking up her mug and intending to walk off. 'Unlike most people here, I don't bring my personal life to work.'

'Whatever the case, I was indiscreet,' Luke said. 'And for that, I apologise.'

His voice was both serious and sincere, so much so that it stilled her, and instead of brushing past him Pippa turned and met his eyes. They were serious and sincere too, and also concerned. She hadn't expected him to follow her, and certainly not to confront things so directly and apologise.

'It's fine,' Pippa said, but she knew there was a raw edge to her voice as she accepted his apology; there was still hurt there. 'Thank you.'

'I knew I remembered you.'

'Well, mystery solved,' she said, forcing a smile as her heart seemed to crumple.

After all, *that* was exactly what hurt, though she didn't want to draw any more attention to it with Luke standing there.

She was back to being Julia's sister all over again.

That conversation in the library—that precious hour which had meant so much to Pippa—had clearly meant nothing to him. He couldn't even recall it.

'I've got to go and do hand-over.'

'Hold on a moment.' He halted her attempt to leave. 'Do you want to catch up?'

'Catch up?'

'I should be finished by six.'

'Are we going to sing the school song?' She attempted a joke, but her voice came out just a little too bitter, and so she checked herself. 'Catch up about what?' she asked, a little bewildered, because his eyes were still on hers, and she had the ridiculous thought that his hand was going to move to her cheek.

The fantasy of him had not just returned, it had been remastered, and it was in full Technicolor now, as she looked into those eyes whose colour she'd once faithfully attempted to capture. Not just Technicolor, though—this fantasy came with the bonus of a citrussy bergamot scent and the bizarre feeling that he was going to take her mug of tea and place it down, so that he might hold her and better apologise with a kiss.

But his next words popped the bubble of hope in which she was floating.

'I don't think work is the place for a private catch-up...'

His voice trailed off and with a sinking feeling Pippa thumped back down to reality. She guessed he wanted to talk about Julia, and her final days.

He hadn't been at the funeral. Her eyes had briefly sought him. In the depths of her grief, she'd wanted just a glimpse of him, to know he was near. Pippa had later heard that he'd gone off on his gap year almost the minute his final exam was over.

His request for more information about Julia

now took her right back to the days, weeks and months after her sister had died—to the funeral, to the endless albeit well-meaning conversations in which people had asked after her parents and pressed her for details as they attempted to probe the family's grief.

Pippa had soon had it down pat.

'They're getting there.'

'She died at home, as she wanted.'

'It was very peaceful.'

That was what she'd said, because it had always seemed the right thing to say.

She hadn't added that she *hoped* it was peaceful—her parents hadn't thought to pull her out of school to give her a chance to say goodbye.

Pippa had felt ill that entire day.

She'd even been to the sick bay and had been given two headache tablets, wishing she could be sent home.

The day had gone on for ever, and when she'd finally got home she'd turned the key in the door with familiar dread to find her aunt standing there.

'Pippa…' her aunt had said, and then she'd guided her into the kitchen.

There, her aunt had told her that just after nine that morning Julia had died.

It had made no sense. While she'd been doing biology, eating lunch, sitting in the library, followed by an art lesson, Julia had been dead…

'Where is she?'

Pippa had turned to run up the stairs, but her aunt had told her that as she'd been walking home from school, her headache pounding, for once not daydreaming about Luke Harris, Julia's body had been being taken away by the undertakers.

She'd never shared that part…nor how her parents had sat on the couch, holding each other and sobbing.

'She's gone…' her mother had said, barely looking up. 'Julia's gone.'

They hadn't followed her when Pippa had gone into Julia's room. Hadn't checked on her as she'd lain on Julia's bed…

Damn you, Luke Harris, for coming to work here and making me remember everything I've tried to forget.

She looked up and saw he was awaiting her response, and even though going for a drink to talk about Julia's death was the last thing she wanted, she certainly did not want to discuss it here. So she ignored the effect of his gaze and the close proximity of him in the small staff kitchen and managed a casual, 'Sure.'

'How about The Avery?' Luke said, naming a nice pub with a great menu that was close to The Primary.

'Sure.'

The Avery was also close enough that she could go home and change, rather than meet him in the jeans she'd worn into work.

That wasn't just vanity.

Just that he was in a gorgeous dark suit with the palest blue shirt.

Okay, it *was* vanity that later had Pippa leafing through her rather boring wardrobe and taking out the nice grey wrap dress she was intending to wear tomorrow for her interview. She moved to put it back, but then, given it was just a quick drink and this was the nicest outfit she had, she decided to wear it.

The dress was versatile—it could be either dressed up with heels and make-up, as it would be tomorrow, or made last-minute smart-casual with boots.

For this evening she chose the latter.

She was soon back on the Underground, on her way to meet him.

For a catch-up.

Breathe...

She wasn't a gawky sixteen-year-old now, with her first crush.

Instead, Pippa reminded herself, she was about to turn thirty, and, if anything, was a little averse to relationships. Anyway, this wasn't a date. Luke just wanted to find out what had happened to Julia.

As the Tube rattled her towards her destination there was time for another honest appraisal.

She liked this.

Going out.

Whether on a date, or out with friends, Pippa

preferred a nice noisy bar where you couldn't really talk too much. It was deeper conversations she avoided—and not just at work, but in all areas of her life…

Still, even if it was Luke Harris, at least she had the conversation down pat.

Died peacefully…yada-yada…

He stood out.

Even in the crowded bar, Pippa saw him straight away. He really was divine, and it made her confident stride falter. If they'd never met—if she'd had no idea who he was—she'd still have noticed him first.

She pushed out a smile and walked over to where he stood at the bar.

'Just in time,' he said. 'What will you have?'

'A grapefruit juice,' she said, and then added, 'Yes, please,' to the offer of ice.

As their drinks were being poured, she glanced around and saw the pub was pretty full, but that there was a high table free in the middle.

'Shall I go and grab it?' Pippa suggested.

'No need.' He shook his head. 'I've got us a place in the lounge,' he said, gesturing beyond. 'It's quieter.'

Her heart sank.

It was indeed quieter.

There were couches and low polished tables that allowed for more intimate conversation. Thankfully he was making his way to some chairs, and Pippa took off her coat, placing it on a hook before taking a seat beside Luke but far enough away to feel opposite to him.

'So,' Pippa said, attempting the dreaded polite small talk, 'you're here for a month?'

He nodded.

'How are you finding it?'

His response was non-committal. 'I'm really just back in London to tie up loose ends.'

'Loose ends?'

'Yes. I want to sell my flat before I head off.'

'Back to America?'

'I'm not sure,' he admitted. 'I was hoping to have a break and get the flat ready to go on the market while I worked out where to go next, but then this offer of a month's work at The Primary came up. It's a great trauma centre, and I couldn't resist... I've left the flat to the estate agent to pretty up.'

'You mean, remove its soul?'

Luke laughed at her perception. 'You could say that. I now have cushions everywhere, as well as rugs I keep tripping over, and this bottle of wine on the counter with two wine glasses and a corkscrew that I'm not allowed to touch.'

'Did they place a cheeseboard in the kitchen?'

'How did you guess?'

'I love looking at houses for sale,' Pippa told him. 'I had vague ideas of being an interior designer once—' she started to say, but then halted, reminding herself that they were here to talk about her sister.

Might as well get it over and done with.

'You wanted to know about Julia?'

He frowned, and she didn't quite know why.

'It was very peaceful,' Pippa told him, and then she gave a practised, reassuring smile. 'She died at home, as she wanted—'

'Pippa.'

He halted her, perhaps a little too abruptly, and in the silence that followed Luke found he was unusually uncertain as to how to proceed. Julia wasn't the reason he had asked her out tonight, but to tell Pippa he wasn't here for a Julia update might sound cold.

Was it cold?

He didn't really know, but there was something he wanted to make very clear.

'I didn't date your sister.'

Her green eyes almost flashed a warning as they met his. 'Yes, Luke, you did.'

'No,' he said. 'I took her to the school dance. That was all.'

'You came over to the house,' Pippa disputed. 'More than a few times.'

'Because she was too unwell to attend the information nights. But we were never dating. Julia wanted to go to the school dance and I was...'

As Luke's voice trailed off she felt foolish as realisation hit. He'd been Head Boy, after all, and no doubt there had been certain duties that came with the role.

'Were you told to ask Julia?'

'It was my pleasure to escort her.'

For someone so arrogant, Pippa thought, he was supremely polite—and his cautious answers gave little away. Yet Pippa wanted clarity.

'But you *were* asked?' she persisted, and he gave a slight nod.

Pippa felt a sudden giddy rush of relief.

They hadn't dated. Luke had just been doing his duty.

'I thought…' She ran a hand through her thick curls, unsure herself how to proceed, and torn because she was still loyal to her sister, who'd clearly had a crush on him too. 'I just assumed the two of you were dating.'

'Pippa…' he said, leaning forward in his chair. He was so tall that, despite the distance between them, their knees and arms brushed. 'I never saw her after the dance. Or visited her in hospital.'

Pippa could feel that she was blushing as he spoke—not just at her own misconceptions but because the heady whoosh of relief she'd felt at the news wasn't abating. If anything, it was heightening…

'I know my relationships are all short lived,' he went on, 'and that at times I can be a bit ruthless, ending things, but even I wouldn't be bastard enough to break up with someone who was terminally ill.'

Pippa blinked as he spoke out loud the words that had been forbidden in her home.

'Sorry.' Pippa reclaimed her knee and moved slightly away, then took a sip of her drink to cover her confusion. It was hard to look back on that time in light of his revelation with him here. 'I was sixteen,' she said. 'I guess at sixteen you think everyone's getting it on.' She gave a hollow laugh. 'Except you.' It was she who frowned now. 'I mean except *me*.'

'I know what you meant,' he said with a smile. 'God, who'd be sixteen again?'

I would, Pippa thought, but didn't say.

The year she'd turned sixteen had been glorious—at least the start of it.

Julia had received her new heart and lungs, and Pippa's birthday and the Christmas that had followed were the happiest weeks Pippa had known. She and Julia had gone Christmas shopping and out for lunch, and then looked at make-up, painting the backs of their hands with lipstick rainbows. Then they'd gone on to a fashionable jewellery shop, where they'd tried on rings neither had been able to afford.

Or so Pippa had thought.

She twisted the silver ring Julia had bought her, which she still wore on her little finger, recalling the bliss of that Christmas Day, when no one had seen the dark clouds gathering and no one had known that the following year everything would change.

And so she got back to the real reason he'd asked her here.

'She died that September,' Pippa said.

'I'd gone on my gap year,' Luke said, nodding, 'but I do remember hearing that she'd died.'

'She'd just found out that she'd got into the university she desperately wanted—St Andrew's.'

There was that swell in her chest again…that rise, that wave, that feeling…but it had nowhere to go. She recalled her sister receiving the wonderful news, the smile on Julia's face, and the shine of pride in her fading eyes.

'She was so pleased to have been accepted. It was her first choice.'

'Oh, yes,' he said, 'that's *such* an achievement. I got my second choice. I was actually hoping for a reason not to be a student with placements at the same hospital as my father, and being accepted at Cambridge would have been a very polite way to bow out…'

She gave a half-laugh, but then realised he was serious. 'You don't get on?'

'I admire his surgical skills.'

And there it was again, the diplomatic response that gave nothing away. But for Pippa it was what he didn't say that spoke volumes.

'So why—?' Pippa halted.

She was usually the least nosy person. And her personal conversations usually dripped like a leaky tap. With Luke, though, it was as if the pipes were shuddering to life. Drip, drip, and then a sudden burst.

'Why did you select it if the two of you weren't getting on?'

'We were getting on fine when the applications went in.' He drained the last of his drink, but instead of heading to the bar, or summoning the waitress, he said, 'My grandfather was a surgeon there…and my father…'

Now Pippa understood what he'd meant in the library when he'd told her his future had been decided even before he was born. She felt a little as if she had a cheat sheet on him, and had to keep remembering to discard what she already knew.

'Still, I really wanted Cambridge. I missed out by a point.'

'Ouch.'

'I ballsed up in the chemistry exam. I can still see the question.' He grimaced. 'Fragmentation…'

Pippa dragged her mind back to her biology lessons, but unlike the library, which she could recall with detail, biology lessons were in the dim past. 'Parent plant?'

'No, that's biology. In chemistry…'

He attempted to explain, but completely lost Pippa along the way.

'Mass spectrometry. Fragmentation.'

'I don't even know what that means!' She groaned at the memory of her science lessons, and especially the homework. 'Chemistry was a nightmare.'

'I liked it. Don't you remember that old chat-up line?' he asked, and she shook her head. 'Excuse me, have you lost an electron? Because you are positively attractive.'

'That's dreadful!' Pippa started to laugh. 'We definitely moved in different circles. I couldn't get past the periodic table.'

Luke smiled. 'Well, I still dream about that damn exam—sitting there, knowing I should know it...' But then his smile faded. 'My head was all over the place,' he admitted. 'My mother wasn't well at the time.'

She watched the column of his throat as he swallowed, the bob of his Adam's apple, and she thought of his red eyes in the library. But she didn't know how to address that—how to discuss a conversation he couldn't even remember.

So she settled for safe. 'St Bede's is a great hospital, though?'

Luke said nothing to that. He just picked up his glass, but then, seeing it was empty, set it down. Clearly he didn't want to prolong the night.

Instead, he got back to being polite. 'So, how have you been since you lost your sister?'

'It's been fourteen years,' Pippa said, but then realised she didn't really know the answer to that question. 'I've been fine, I guess.'

'How about your parents?'

'They're...' It would take more than the dregs of her grapefruit juice to tell him about that. 'They're well.'

'So why are you avoiding them?' He wagged a finger. 'Don't forget, I heard you on the phone.'

Pippa gave a wry laugh at both the memory and his perception. 'Okay, fine…they're not doing so well. They've never moved on from it and I doubt they ever will.'

'It must be hard…'

'Of course, losing a child—'

'I meant it must be hard on *you*.'

Oh.

Pippa hadn't been expecting that. Seriously had not been expecting that. Because since Julia's death, most people only asked about her parents.

She didn't know how to respond, but her silence didn't stop Luke.

'So how come you haven't told anyone at work about Julia?'

'It's just…never come up.' Pippa shrugged, but she saw the frown that said he didn't believe her.

He wasn't wrong. She was a nurse on a paediatric ward, and her colleagues were friendly.

'I haven't worked there for long.'

'How long?'

'Two years…'

'I rest my case.'

She actually laughed.

'And then I went and put my foot in it.'

'Not really,' Pippa said. 'I guess it came out naturally. I mean…' She took a tense breath. 'I just don't like talking about it.'

There was a stretch of silence, and she let it hang there to see whether he would fill it.

He chose not to. Fair enough.

Their drinks were empty, the subject of Julia had been covered—well, not really—but just when she expected the evening to end, Luke picked up the menus and handed her one.

'I thought we were only having a drink?'

'Just a drink?' He frowned. 'At six in the evening? I don't know about you, but I'm starving. Anyway, like I said, I didn't think work was the right place for a private catch-up.' He gave a wry smile. 'Not that we've ever properly met...'

Pippa took a breath and told herself to simply let it go. She was annoyed with herself that it still hurt this much. That he couldn't remember their short conversation was a ridiculous reason to take offence, and yet she still felt slighted.

'We have met,'

'Oh?' He put his head slightly to the side. 'So you *were* on the swimming team?'

'No.' Pippa shook her head and laughed ruefully. 'You helped me choose my A-level subjects.'

Watching his eyes narrow as he tried to recall something that had meant everything to her—and clearly *only* to her—hurt so much it felt almost like a physical pain.

'We were in the library...?' she persisted.

He shook his head.

'The day you asked—' She corrected herself. 'The day you were asked to take Julia to the dance?'

* * *

Luke frowned, and not just because he was trying to place her. There was a flicker of a long-ago memory lying just beyond his reach. He hadn't wanted to take Julia to the dance; he hadn't even wanted to go himself. He'd have rather been studying. But for other reasons entirely the school dance had been the last thing on his mind that day.

He'd found out his father was cheating.

A couple of weeks away from important exams, racing home during a study period to grab his forgotten swimming gear, he'd found out that his father wasn't so perfect after all.

'*Get her out!*' he'd screamed at his father.

After the woman had gone, he'd demanded, '*Who is she?*'

'*It doesn't matter.*'

'*It doesn't* matter?' Luke had roared.

'*I mean it's nothing serious.*'

That had only enraged Luke further, and the argument that had followed had almost turned physical.

'*You've got everything!*' Luke had shouted. '*How the hell could you throw it all away?*'

'*I'm not throwing anything away,*' his father, Matthew, had said placatingly. '*Luke, you have no idea...*'

He changed tack then and followed up with, '*Your mother doesn't need to know.*'

'*I am* not *keeping this from her. Either you tell her, or I will,*' Luke had warned him.

And, grabbing his sports bag, he'd raced back to school.

His father hadn't told her, of course.

His delightfully dizzy, always vague mother had been all smiles when he'd stepped through the front door after school.

'Darling you're home...' She'd given him a kiss. *'Luke, you simply must call Julia. I know you've got homework, but no more putting it off.'*

And so he'd called Julia and asked her to the dance, but his temper had been bubbling beneath the surface the whole time. Once he'd ended the call, his disgust had returned in full force—not just at the deceit, but at the fact that his father would bring his lover into the family home.

'Don't sulk, Luke,' his mother had scolded him lightly. *'The poor girl needs something to look forward to.'*

'I'm not sulking,' he'd said, and when she'd headed into the lounge, he'd looked at his father. *'I'm going for a walk. If you haven't told her by the time I get back, then I will.'*

He'd had no idea what he'd return to.

Flashing blue lights in the driveway.

His mother being stretchered away.

Luke hadn't been able to understand how willing his mother had been to throw it all away either. He still didn't.

He'd not only sworn off marriage that day, he'd vowed that, apart from at work, he would never let anyone be that reliant on him.

Luke didn't want to return to his memories of that time—and certainly not on a Monday night in The Avery. So he looked at Pippa, who was insistent that they'd spoken in the library.

'I don't remember,' he admitted, and then got back to his charming self. 'Do you want some wine?'

'Sure,' she said quietly.

'Red, white…? Or champagne, given it's a reunion?'

Pippa was tempted to point out that it wasn't much of a reunion if one person had no memory of meeting the other, but she knew she had to let that go or nurse it in private.

That reminded her… 'I thought you wanted to talk privately…?'

'I do,' Luke agreed. '*You're* the reason I wasn't eating in the consultants' lounge.'

Pippa swallowed and frantically looked at the menu, trying to make sense of his words. Was he saying that he'd come to the ward to see *her*?

'That's why I suggested we come here. I'm sure you'd rather your colleagues don't get wind that there's anything going on between us.'

'There *isn't* anything going on between us,' Pippa said sharply.

Only when she dared to glance up he looked as unconvinced by her statement as she felt.

'Are you sure about that?' Luke checked.

His question was too direct to avoid. 'No…' Pippa admitted.

'Good,' he responded, then gestured to the menu. 'Have you chosen?'

He expected her to choose what to eat after *that*?

'The chicken Provençal.'

He screwed up his gorgeous straight nose. 'I wouldn't have that here.'

'Have you tried it?'

'No,' Luke admitted, 'but if I'm eating French then I want an arrogant French chef preparing it. There's a restaurant near me… You can hear Anton cursing in the background.'

Pippa laughed.

'And the waiters and waitresses all speak only French and pretend not to understand your attempts to communicate. I swear, it's agony…'

'It sounds dreadful.'

'Ah, but so worth it.'

'Well, I'll have the Greek lamb salad, then,' Pippa said, 'and I don't care if it's not authentic.'

Luke had steak with salad, but no chips, and ordered a bottle of red wine, which felt very decadent for a week day.

'Philadelphia was incredible,' he told her as they began to talk about work. 'I think it's the most beautiful city I've ever seen. It has its problems, of course—and that's why I went there, for the experience. I just wasn't expecting to love it so much.'

'I've never been to America,' Pippa said with a sigh. 'It's on my list. I want to go to Colorado.'

'Well, add Philadelphia to that list.'

'So, was it always the plan? To study in the States?'

'Not at all.' He topped up their glasses. 'There's no clear path for a trauma surgeon in the UK.'

'Really?'

'For post-grad qualifications you have to go to the States or South Africa.'

'Why, when there's so much trauma here?'

'Exactly! And when they get around to making a clearly defined role, I'll be ready.'

He shrugged and smiled that slightly arrogant smile that made her knees weak.

'I'm taking a break after The Primary. I'm going to the Outer Hebrides. I want to see a Scottish winter, and certainly no trauma.'

'I wouldn't be so sure. You'll be on air and sea rescue, or something.'

Luke opened his mouth to correct her—to tell Pippa that he wasn't going to Scotland to work. Nor even to avoid the agony of playing Happy Families on Christmas Day with his parents and enduring the endless questions from his mother and sister as to when he'd settle down.

No, he was getting away for a much-needed break.

While he loved his job, Luke was self-aware enough to know that he needed time away. The horror of broken, damaged bodies took its toll— he'd accepted that. But lately the hell of breaking bad news, of watching families fall apart before his eyes, had found him wondering not just about whether his patient would make it, but also, with the uphill battle ahead, would their loved ones survive…?

But he hadn't discussed it with anyone, and he wasn't about to bring the mood down now.

He looked at Pippa's soft dark curls, and though this gentleman generally *did* prefer tall, leggy blondes, he thought Pippa Westford might just be changing his mind. Even when she'd been dressed in unflattering scrubs he'd noticed that she was gorgeous, but he'd underestimated quite how much. Her dress affirmed soft curves, and her pale skin flushed easily and told him more than her guarded green eyes.

She intrigued him. There was an air of independence about her, and when combined with a certain restraint it was a stunning mixture.

Their meals arrived—including chips, instead of the salad Luke had ordered. But he didn't comment, just thanked the waiter.

'Won't you miss London?' asked Pippa.

'No.' He gave a very definite shake of his head. 'That's not to say I'm not enjoying my time here.' He looked right at her then. 'And now.'

He meant them.

This.

Here and now.

She could feel the energy between them.

Now that she knew the truth about him and her sister, she could allow herself to feel it…to look back into his velvety eyes, to enjoy him—enjoy *this*—and to feel those eyes drifting to her lips.

She looked at him. Whatever she felt here and now, he was just passing through—or rather, tying up loose ends so that he could leave.

'Isn't it nice to have a base here, though. Couldn't you rent your apartment out?'

'That's what I've been doing, but it's in a very old building and always needing maintenance. It's too much commitment—and I don't need a base here.'

'But your family—' She halted. 'Sorry, that's none of my business.'

Usually Luke would have taken up her polite offer and shut that line of conversation down. He *never* discussed his family—or at least he kept his responses to questions about them minimal and superficial.

Luke didn't even discuss family with his family…

Not any more.

'How could you, Luke?' his mother had asked two years ago.

As vague and dizzy as she'd appeared at times, she'd known all the theatre staff and all the goings-on at St Bede's, and his sister, Anna, worked there in the ED. When it had all blown up, and Shona's husband had been placed on stress leave, Hannah

Harris had looked up at her son, white with fury, but with tears in her eyes.

'I thought you of all people would know better,' she'd sneered. *'Like father, like son.'*

He'd gone to the States, and now he was back, it seemed that all was forgotten. The dust had settled.

Luke still couldn't forgive his father, though.

'It's fine,' Luke said in response to Pippa's apology. 'After all, I just asked about your family. Like you, I'd prefer not to talk about it.'

He gave her a smile that had her stomach feeling as if it were made of jelly, though not in a jiggly, fat way…more as if her insides were wobbling in response to his smile and the darkness of his eyes.

'Have a chip.' He changed the subject and pushed forward his plate. 'You know you want to.'

Pippa smiled—only it wasn't her usual smile. It was a new smile. And she knew that to be the case because there was an unfamiliar feeling of her top lip stretching, or pressing, or pouting… She honestly wasn't sure what it was doing. It was, she deduced, the smile she wore when she was sitting in The Avery with Luke and flirting.

She wasn't a flirty person.

Usually.

Yet here she was, pushing her half-empty plate forward to allow him to stab an olive. Usually Pippa didn't share her food—didn't share anything, really. Not her deep thoughts, not her emotions, and certainly not what was on her plate…

Things felt different with him.

They chatted so easily. She even told him about her tiny flat a couple of stops on the Tube from where they were.

'Is it a flat-share?'

'Gosh, no.' Pippa shook her head. 'I'm way past that.'

'How old are you?'

'Twenty-nine,' Pippa told him. 'But I gave up sharing the day I finished university. I like my own space too much. What about yours?' Pippa asked. 'Is it on the market?'

'As of today, it is. I'm hoping it will be snapped up; I really don't want to be here too long…'

'I thought people ran away *to* London?'

'Who said anything about running away?'

'No one. I…um… I…'

For the first time the conversation faltered, and she stammered over her words, but she was rescued by someone coming to clear their plates.

Luke must have noticed, because as he topped up their wine he addressed her awkwardness. 'You've heard the gossip?'

'I try not to listen, but…' Pippa flushed. 'God knows I hate it when they gossip about me.'

'About you?' His eyes widened. 'Do tell!'

'That's just it; there's nothing to tell. But because I don't drag my personal life into work they assume I'm frigid…or a lesbian…'

'An interesting combination,' he mused. 'I'd love to debunk both assumptions…'

He gave her such a wicked smile that Pippa couldn't help but laugh.

'So what have you heard about me?' he asked.

'Just the usual. I know I shouldn't listen, but it's hard not to at the moment—you're the talk of The Primary.' She pushed out a smile. 'Breaking hearts wherever you go.'

'Incorrect,' he said, shaking his head. 'I don't get overly involved with anyone and, given I make that crystal-clear from the get-go, nobody gets hurt.'

He must have seen her tiny frown, because he went on.

'That rumour you've heard about a married woman is false. For one thing, I would never get in the middle of someone's relationship.'

'And for another?' Pippa was pushing for more information because she had a burning curiosity to know him more.

'I loathe cheats.'

'Fair enough.' She took a sip of her wine.

'Are *you* seeing anyone, Pippa?'

His enquiry was direct. The preamble that had lulled her seemed to have shifted, and like a skilled interrogator he'd caught her unaware with the simplest of questions.

Pippa held her wine in her mouth, knowing her response mattered.

Yes, she wanted to say, even though it would be a complete and utter lie.

But, given what he'd just told her, it would keep the lion in its cage.

Yes, she was tempted to say, *I am seeing someone*.

Because then they would go their separate ways....

Yes, she decided to say as she swallowed her wine.

It was a single word that failed her.

'No,' Pippa responded, and shook her head. 'I'm not seeing anyone.'

'You're sure about that?' Luke checked.

Given her delay in responding, his question was merited.

'Quite sure,' Pippa said, nodding, and then added, 'I'm not brilliant at long-term relationships.'

Their eyes held and she saw the same flare she had seen there on his first day at The Primary— only she knew now that it was desire. It was at that moment when Pippa realised she might have given a false impression and made it sound as if she preferred short-term flings.

What she'd meant was that even though she wasn't good at long-term, she always went into a relationship with hope. Hope that this time things might be different…hope that she might finally be able to open up and truly be herself with another.

It had never worked out, though. Because she always felt a certain sense of threat as things turned more serious. She was coming to accept that she didn't like people getting too close. She didn't even like getting in touch with her own feelings, let alone allowing someone else in.

Last orders were called, and Pippa blinked when she saw the time—the evening had flown by.

'Excuse me a moment.'

It was a relief to escape to the loo. She stood in front of the mirror and took a breath, trying to digest what he'd said about never dating Julia.

She'd been frozen in her teenage mind where Luke and her sister were concerned, and it felt exhilarating to be freed from the misconception that her parents perpetuated even to this day.

Pippa took a shaky breath, almost feeling the years peeling away. Yes, she liked him still. Of course she did. But in a different way. Fourteen years ago her unblemished, innocent heart had believed in silver dresses and being swept away in his arms... That was all she'd dreamt of really...and perhaps a kiss...

Now, her rather bruised heart knew there was more to it.

Luke Harris was here for a month and no more. He'd made it clear so that she understood this was going nowhere. He was a player, not a partner. Pippa understood his terms.

But the trouble wasn't just keeping the lion caged. Rather, it was the lioness inside her, pawing to get out...

Pippa wanted to know true passion, and she wanted to douse the torch she still carried for Luke Harris.

But wasn't she too serious for a casual fling, though? It simply wasn't her...

And yet that heady gush of relief that he hadn't dated Julia *still* hadn't abated.

Pippa caught sight of herself in the mirror. Her hair was tousled and the grey interview dress somehow looked indecent as it clung to her breasts. Those boring army-green eyes were no more. Now they were black with unfamiliar desire...

She thought of her sister and wished she could call her and ask for advice.

But then she realised she already knew Julia's take on life.

Julia had lived her life as if it wasn't ending.

If her sister could study for straight As, knowing there was little prospect of going to university, let alone making use of the grades, then surely she could live the same way...

Julia had grabbed life and taken every opportunity she was offered—smiling and happy, seemingly carefree—squeezing every last drop out of life all the while knowing it would be over too soon.

Julia had lived her entire life without the promise of a future, she realised. Surely she, Pippa, could manage a month.

If Julia could do it...

'Then so can you,' Pippa told her reflection.

Less than a month, she amended, as she made her way back to the table, given he'd been at The Primary a full week now.

The table had been cleared, the bill paid...

'Ready?' he said, and Pippa nodded and put on her coat.

It had rained while they were in the pub. Now, cars and buses swished past, their headlights casting light tails, the beams from streetlamps highlighting the heavy drops that still fell. They stood under cover and faced each other.

'Thanks for dinner,' Pippa said. 'I had a great night.'

'It hasn't finished yet.'

He took her face in his hands and with his velvet-soft lips he kissed her…incredibly slowly.

It was everything she had ever thought it would be.

Actually, it was better—and not just because it was real.

As his tongue slipped in, she could taste the wine they had shared, only it seemed sharper and more potent, and the soft stroking of his tongue evoked a different, unfamiliar type of hunger…

Luke Harris had been her teenage dream, but now he was here, and he was kissing her, and she did not want to let the dream go.

Not just yet…

She thought of her sister—how she'd lived without fear, following her goals and passions.

And that made her brave.

Their kiss ended, but his hands were still cupping her face. She wanted to run her tongue over her lips, if only to taste him again.

'We could have a very nice month, Pippa…'

A month.

Perhaps she should feel offended that he'd named

the end date of their affair as it was only just bursting into life, but instead it sent a shiver of excitement through her.

No promises that could never be kept.

No false hope.

Just a chance to live her dream.

And no recriminations over her refusal to open up her heart.

Luke didn't want that part of her.

Wanton and emboldened, she released the lioness.

'So,' Pippa said, 'are you going to show me this flat of yours?'

CHAPTER FOUR

LONDON LOOKED ALL SHINY, as if wiped clean by the rain.

'Right you are,' said the taxi driver, when Luke gave him their destination. 'That was some storm!'

'We didn't see it,' Luke said, and turned to resume their kiss.

But the driver had other ideas. 'All the traffic lights went out and…'

He carried on talking and didn't seem to require a response.

Pippa felt all shiny too, like the city, and she was laughing at the press of Luke's hand, and the nudge of his knee, because they'd somehow landed the chattiest taxi driver in the world.

They passed St Bede's, the gorgeous old hospital with its beautiful arches, and then turned down a very narrow cobbled street. This was old, old London, Pippa thought, as Luke paid the taxi driver. His apartment building was very close to the hospital. He'd really had a whole life here, and it bemused her that he could so readily leave it all behind.

Why?

It wasn't as if he denied his reputation—indeed, he seemed at ease with it. Why would he run from some rumour he'd said was false? It didn't equate to the confident, self-assured man who now moved up the steps with her to the heavy entrance doors of the building. As he opened them up, she glanced at a row of doorbells and saw *LH* near the top.

'It's quite a climb,' Luke warned, as he led them into the foyer.

Pippa looked up at the gorgeous swirl of a circular stone staircase with polished banisters, and as she gazed higher, to the incredible domed skylight, he caught her unawares and lowered his head to kiss her throat. His mouth found hers and he guided her to the wall, never breaking the kiss for a second.

'Sustenance,' he said as his hand slid inside her coat and pulled her hips against his. 'We could have a *very* nice month,' he said again, lifting her hair and kissing the side of her neck.

'It's only three weeks,' Pippa gasped, as he pulled her so close that she could feel how turned on her was.

'Haven't you enjoyed it so far?' Luke asked, kissing her as she had secretly wanted him to.

'Yes...'

'So, a month,' he said.

But then they heard footsteps and politely parted, Luke nodding and smiling to a woman who passed them with the cutest little dachshund puppy.

'Hi, Luke,' she said as she passed.

'Hey,' he said. As she opened the door and took the little dog outside, Luke rolled his eyes at Pippa. 'Can you believe she called him Sausage?'

'It's cute.'

'She hardly put a lot of thought into—'

'I think,' Pippa suggested, 'we should go up before she gets back.'

'Agreed.'

They almost flew up the stairs in their mutual race to get to the top, but they held hands the whole way, unable to drop contact. It was as though they were tied together in some new version of a three-legged race.

Not once had she felt like this—laughing, practically running up flights of stairs just to get behind closed doors. Never had she felt so at ease at the prospect of sleeping with a man for the first time.

He opened a large dark door and as he kissed her and moved them inside he shrugged off his coat, then slowly removed Pippa's.

He showered her with kisses that made her breathless as they attempted to undress each other. The bedroom was apparently too far away and buttons were too complicated.

She felt the roughness of his unshaven chin and the probing of his tongue, and there was the ever-present thrum of demand as his kiss changed tempo and they sank to the hardwood floor.

Pippa kissed him back hard, more passionately than she'd thought herself capable of, lost for a moment in the bliss of him. His hands were parting her dress, pulling at her opaque tights, and she lifted her hips with the same urgency his hands communicated. It was Pippa who was pulling her tights and knickers down as he slipped a condom on. She attempted to pull off her boots, but they were too desperate for intimate contact to negotiate even that.

'Ow!' he said as her closed knees pressed into his stomach, but neither of them cared.

'Yes…' she moaned as he pulled her hips down onto him and ground into her. 'Oh, my…'

She must have the female equivalent of premature ejaculation, she thought, because she was starting to come. Not that it mattered; Luke was more than ready to reciprocate.

Her hands were flat on his chest, and she was enjoying the delicious sight of Luke coming. One breast was exposed, her tights were wound like a lasso around her thighs, and he was still inside her…

She was panting, stunned at her own body's rapid response. His hand was on her red cheek as she now attempted to gulp in air.

'Bed,' Luke said, in a voice that told her they'd only just started.

CHAPTER FIVE

'MORNING,' LUKE SAID lazily as his phone bleeped them awake. At least, it had bleeped him awake. Perhaps used to being summoned immediately, he propelled himself to sit up. 'Do you have to be at work?'

'No…' Pippa, still half dozing, tried to peel her eyes open, then remembered she'd fallen asleep in her contact lenses and promptly closed them. 'I'm not back till tomorrow.'

'So you're off today?' he asked, already up and out of bed.

'Mmm…although I've got—'

She stopped herself from telling him about her interview this morning. Because this interview, even if she was trying to play it down to herself, was the most important of her life.

She wanted this job.

It was everything she wanted in her career.

So it didn't make for good idle conversation with a new lover.

Pippa had thought about telling him about the interview. Simply because he was wise. It was an odd thing, to stare at a self-confessed playboy who was just passing through and think about how wise he was.

But he was the one who had talked about how he didn't like to get involved. Surely that kind of conversation would be the definition of *involved*?

Talking about the interview would also mean mentioning Julia, and she couldn't do that without crying.

Which would not be a good look at six a.m. after their first night together.

'Got what?' Luke persisted, with a yawn.

'Places I need to be.'

Her response was evasive—the perfect casual lover reply. She peeled her itchy eyes open and wished for twenty/twenty vision, because the sight of a naked Luke stretching and yawning was one she'd rather not have missed!

'Were you in the army?' she asked.

'No—why?'

'I've never seen anyone get up so fast.'

'If I hit snooze…' He shook his head. 'It's a dangerous path. Especially as I've got seven a.m. ward rounds,' he added 'Coffee?' he offered.

'Please.' Pippa nodded as he wrapped a towel around his waist before striding into the lounge. 'Two sugars!' she called to his departing and very attractive back. 'White.'

Sitting up, she shivered and pulled at the throw blanket placed over the headboard. She wrapped it around her bare shoulders, then blinked as the world according to Luke came into focus.

She looked at the rumpled bed with its navy sheets and pillows that she hadn't really noticed last night. Then she gazed at the polished hardwood floors, whose beauty was hidden beneath too many scattered rugs, then up to the very high ceiling, with its cornices and intricate central ceiling rose spoilt by a surprisingly modern light. Above the very beautiful and rather neglected fireplace was a very large print of two buses in Oxford Street; it seemed a rather odd choice for a bedroom.

'Awful, isn't it?' Luke said as he came back into the bedroom with two mugs. 'The estate agent's handiwork, to cover some bumps in the walls. Did you see the one he put up in the lounge?'

'I wasn't really paying attention,' Pippa said, laughing. 'You could dress up the fireplace instead of covering up the walls,' she added. She looked at the huge windows, and then up again at the ceiling. 'And a chandelier in here would be nice.'

'In a bedroom?'

'A small one.' Pippa nodded her thanks as he handed her a mug.

'Sorry, I don't have any milk.'

'It's fine,' Pippa said. 'Your flat is even colder than mine.'

'I've put the heating on, though it takes for ever. I'm meant to leave it on all day.'

'Why?'

'Potential buyers,' he said, sighing. 'Not my idea…' He looked at her and smiled. 'That blanket you're wearing is for display purposes only.'

'Oh? And there I was thinking how thoughtful you were,' Pippa teased. Taking a sip of her coffee, she screwed up her nose and placed it on the bed-side table, deciding to stop at her favourite coffee shop on the way home. 'I'm going to get going,' she said.

'Have a shower?' he offered. 'I'm going to.'

He gave her a smile that invited her to join him, but all her bravado from last night seemed to have left.

'I'll wait till I'm home.'

'Pity,' he said.

Pippa bit her lip. She wanted to ask when they might see each other again, but didn't want to sound needy.

So, instead of making a complete fool of herself by asking, or following him into the shower as she'd *really* like to, Pippa got dressed, and was just putting in some fresh contact lenses, which she always kept in her purse, just in case, when he came out.

'I don't sleep in them usually,' Pippa told him, trying to ignore his big, damp body as he hastily dried it. 'I'd really better get going.'

'Pippa!' He called her back. 'I'm on call for the next few nights, and I don't know how busy I'm going to be. I might not be the best company for a while.'

'It's fine.'

'Come on, Pip, give me your number.'

He'd called her that again, not noticing the press of her lips as he took out his phone.

She couldn't quite believe she'd slept with someone who didn't even know her phone number.

But she knew that was the game she'd signed up for, Pippa thought as they exchanged contact details, and she shook it off as she closed the door of his flat behind her.

And she knew something else—something she dared not admit…

She'd only ever have dared to play this game with him.

Pippa wished she'd taken Nola up on her offer of a mock interview, because the real one wasn't going very well.

'Philippa?'

She'd been introduced to a panel of three people.

'Pippa Westford,' she had said, shaking hands with the formidable trio.

One, Miss Brett, had been the manager of a hospice Pippa had once worked at, although clearly she didn't recall Pippa, because despite her initial correction she kept calling her Philippa.

Pippa had intended to wear the grey dress, but after last night it needed a trip to the dry cleaner's, so she wore a navy suit and low heels instead. She had straightened her wild hair and put it up and, while she knew she looked smart, she feared she didn't sound it!

The first part had been okay…*ish*. Pippa had been given an imagined scenario: an anorexic thirteen-year-old who had taken an overdose but was too acutely unwell to be admitted to Psych—or rather to the new eating disorder unit that would be opening in the new wing.

It had all gone downhill from there.

She'd been expecting a question about how she dealt with conflict, but instead of asking about conflicts with patients or parents, they'd just asked about conflict between colleagues.

'I generally get on well with my colleagues,' Pippa responded, and then kicked herself, because it was a pretty poor effort. 'I always try to see the other side.'

'But as Unit Manager you won't be able to sit on the fence,' Miss Brett pointed out.

Later, she would blame it on lack of sleep, or the night spent with Luke, but she knew that would just be making excuses.

'What do you think you can bring to the PAC Unit, Philippa?'

'Well, I've worked in a lot of different areas. Not just on general wards—I've worked on Oncology, in a hospice, as well as on a renal unit.'

'Yes…' One of the trust directors looked at her sternly. 'You've moved around quite a bit.'

'I have,' Pippa agreed, hearing the slight barb behind the words.

It was true; she had moved around rather a lot. A year here, eighteen months there, two years now at The Primary…

'I'm very happy at The Primary. I just feel…' Her voice trailed off.

She'd been so logical in making the decision to apply, but logic seemed to have gone out of the window since Luke's return. Old wounds were resurfacing, and an interview wasn't the place to rip off the plaster and express the raw feelings that were churning inside her. 'I think that my experience, though varied, is all appropriate for the PAC Unit.'

'What would you like to achieve?'

This one Pippa *had* prepared for!

'A higher-level management role, eventually, but—'

'I meant for the PAC Unit,' Miss Brett said, and Pippa realised she'd misunderstood the question. 'What goals would you set for the PAC Unit?'

Pippa stumbled through the rest of the interview and knew she'd done dreadfully, though it was all pleasant handshakes and 'Thank you for your time,' when it concluded.

As Pippa made her way down the corridor to head for home, she saw Nola.

'How did it go?'

'Awful.' Pippa rolled her eyes. 'There's a reason I didn't want to tell anyone I was applying. I flunked it.'

'Don't worry,' Nola said kindly. 'I won't breathe a word.'

Pippa didn't believe her for a moment.

The day only went downhill from there.

Luke didn't so much as text.

Rather than waiting for him to call, Pippa kept busy, and even went over to her parents' house—something she'd been putting off.

'I thought you'd be here earlier,' her mother reprimanded as soon as she came in. 'It's been ages since you've been to the cemetery.'

'I might try and go in the week,' Pippa said as she took off her coat. 'Hi, Dad.' She gave him a kiss. 'Or on my birthday.'

'That's weeks away.'

'It's two weeks away. I'm on an early shift,' she ventured, just in case they were planning anything.

Sure, Pippa thought wryly. *As if they would.*

Birthdays were practically a *verboten* subject, and Christmas remained a teary affair.

And even though Pippa was trying not to think about Luke, even at her parents' there was no chance of escape, because there on the mantelpiece was that photo of Julia and Luke, staring back at her.

'You'll never guess who's working at The Primary,' Pippa began.

'Who?' her mother asked.

Yet even as she opened her mouth to respond, she glanced at the picture and knew it would upset them. 'Miss Brett. I worked with her at the hospice.'

Her mother stared at her blankly.

'Briefly,' Pippa amended. 'She was the manager there. She's one of the big bosses at the hospital now. I had an interview today and she was on the panel.'

'That's nice.'

Conversation with her parents felt like hitting the 'Print' button, knowing full well that the printer was switched off, or out of paper, or not within range.

There was no enquiry as to how her interview had gone, let alone any interest in what it might have been for.

Just the usual, 'That's nice.'

Thank goodness she had the excuse of having to leave to get to her art class. She stopped on the way and brought wine, as well as some crackers and cheese, and she felt the familiar relief as she stepped in to the studio.

The same relief she'd felt in the art room at school.

Tonight it was open studio time, and although Pippa had intended to work on her charcoal sketching she found herself mixing oils instead, with the wine and cheese forgotten. She was soon absorbed.

'What are you working on, Pippa?' asked her teacher, Cassie.

'Light beams.' Pippa looked at her effort, thinking back to last night, and how the car lights had reflected on the wet streets, but also how she'd felt as she stepped into the adventure. 'I can't seem to capture them, though...'

The same way she could never capture Luke.

Pippa knew better than to dream, or even try to hold on to him. It would be easier to hold light in her hand.

She didn't regret their night together, even if she wasn't usually that bold or effervescent.

She was, Pippa knew, too serious by far.

A little dreary, even.

Yet last night she'd felt golden and bright and, yes, for the first time, a little radiant, and she wanted more of the same…

As the teacher guided her to blur the lines, to be bolder with her strokes, Pippa watched her work start to come alive.

'Just have fun with it!' Cassie suggested playfully, and moved on to the next student.

Pippa looked at the shimmering lines she'd created, proud of her work, and took a breath, replaying Cassie's words but with Luke in mind…

'Just have fun with it…'

CHAPTER SIX

Pippa woke up the next morning annoyed that not only was she thinking of Luke, she had even dreamt of him!

And that was *so* not Pippa.

It hadn't been a sexy dream, or anything like that... In truth, as she took the Tube to work, Pippa couldn't really remember what it had been about. She simply wasn't used to having another person so constantly in her thoughts.

And while last night she'd felt emboldened as she'd painted, now she was back to wondering if she had what it took for a casual fling.

It was all very well to 'just have fun with it', but Pippa knew she still needed to guard her heart.

She stopped for her regular coffee and chatted to the barista while it was being made.

'We had a food truck on the river for Diwali last night,' Rohan explained as he made her milky brew. 'You know—the festival of light.'

'One of the mums at work told me about it.' Pippa nodded. 'I should go and have a look.'

'Do,' Rohan agreed, putting the lid on her coffee. 'They're lighting up the London Eye in the colours of the Rangoli tonight.'

'Sounds wonderful. I will go!' Pippa said, collecting her drink and dashing off, because she really didn't want to be late for work.

Very deliberately she didn't pause to look at the

brand-new extension. She was still disappointed at how the interview had gone yesterday. Even though her ward would be moving into the new wing, it was the PAC Unit that she wanted, and she was certain she'd blown it.

Oh, why hadn't she asked Nola for help in preparing?

She was mulling over that, rather than Luke, as she walked down the corridor, overheating in her long scarf, when she heard his voice.

'Excuse me, have you lost an electron?'

Pippa laughed. 'That really is the worst line. And I know I'm not positively attractive this morning.'

'Me neither.'

Pippa chose not to debate the point—he was wearing navy scrubs and had a theatre cap tied on, and he was looking incredibly sexy.

'What did you get up to last night?' he asked.

'I had my art class,' Pippa said. 'Well, *class* might be stretching it a bit. Really it's a weekly "Paint and Sip…"' He frowned, but there wasn't time to elaborate, and anyway she wasn't sure how to play this. 'I'm late…'

'Not too late to stop for coffee,' he pointed out.

'They know my usual order,' she said, and couldn't help adding, 'And they always have milk!'

Instead of responding to her little jibe he said, 'Can I steal it?'

'Not a chance.'

'Seriously… I'm dead on my feet. Just a few

ward rounds and then I'm crashing—hopefully until tomorrow.'

'Busy night?'

'Yes.' He nodded, but didn't elaborate, because his pager went off then—and not just his pager, but the overhead chimes too, asking for the trauma team to come to ED. 'Damn,' Luke said, looking at his pager. 'Multi-trauma on its way.'

It was a horrible time to be called—just before the pagers had been handed over to the day team—but it happened all too often.

'Here,' she said, handing over her precious brew, then rolled her eyes at herself as he took it and sped off.

Honestly, there wasn't anyone else she'd have done that for.

Not that he could ever know that, Pippa told herself, determined to keep things light between them, to be the woman she'd hoped to be—the one who grabbed life...

She walked on to the children's ward, and had barely taken off her scarf before Jenny chimed up. 'So, you've applied for the Unit Manager position on the PAC?'

So much for Nola's discretion. Pippa just rolled her eyes again and headed to the kitchen to make a horrible cup of the hospital's instant coffee, still surprised she'd given her own away—even to Luke.

Thank God Pippa had given him her coffee.

It was warm, sickly sweet, and nothing like the

strong black he preferred, but it was incredibly welcome after a long night that wasn't even about to end soon, judging by the alerts coming in regarding a major RTA—Road Traffic Accident.

Fiona arrived, breathless from her run through the hospital, just as May, the ED Nurse Manager, was giving a briefing, giving the staff the latest update from the scene.

The accident was on the A4, and although there were other hospitals closer, some casualties were being flown in by helicopter or driven with lights and sirens to The Primary, which was a major trauma centre and covered a vast area.

'There are eight casualties in total; we're accepting three.' May held up three fingers to the gathered teams. 'First one's a traumatic chest. Med flight eight minutes. Gino's got him.'

Luke knew there were teams already at the helipad. Gino, one of the senior surgeons from the first on team for the day, would take care of this young man from one of vehicles, though as the patient was wheeled into Resus, Luke could see he didn't look good.

'Go and assist,' Luke told Fiona—and not just because they were short-staffed. Fiona needed the experience, and David, Luke's registrar, had just arrived.

A second patient was rushed past, screaming for her children. She had a displaced hip and, from what Luke could see, a nasty lower leg fracture.

The emergency team took over her care and then

May pointed to Luke as he drained the last of Pippa's coffee. 'Four-year-old male, multi-trauma, unconscious. ETA five minutes. I'll go and meet him.'

As she went to meet the patient Luke began checking drugs as the nursing team set up for a paediatric trauma patient. Remi, the anaesthetist, was selecting various-sized endotracheal tubes, preparing for all possibilities.

When he came, it was clear that the patient was small. It was the first thing Luke noticed as the paramedics wheeled the stretcher in—as well as the fact he'd already been intubated at the scene.

'Darcy!' The paramedic said the child's name very specifically, and soon Luke understood why. 'Identical twin...'

The grim features of the paramedics and trauma team told Luke that what they'd seen had been upsetting. He didn't ask about the other twin, deliberately keeping his focus solely on the patient he had.

'He's four?' Luke checked. The information was important for drug doses and such.

'No, turned five last week,' he was told by the paramedic.

A doctor who'd happened to be on the scene described the life-saving procedures that had been performed. 'Hypovolemic shock, became bradycardic...cardiac massage commenced, then intubated.'

His pyjamas had been cut open, revealing a skinny frame and a distended abdomen which Luke palpated and then percussed, tapping it and eliciting dull sounds that indicated fluid. When the anaesthetist confirmed the airway inserted on scene was patent and secured, the boy was carefully rolled and examined. Luke made the decision to get him straight to CT, and if that wasn't clear then up to Theatre.

'Is CT ready for him?' he called out to May, who came in then. 'Or is the other patient still…?'

'It's clear,' she said, and shook her head.

When Fiona appeared, coming to assist him, Luke knew the young man must have died.

'They're ready,' May said. 'I've let them know you're on your way.'

They were indeed waiting, and soon images were coming through that, mercifully, showed no sign of serious head injury. But his torso had taken the blunt force, and he had a ruptured spleen and a lacerated kidney; this little boy needed Theatre now.

'Let's get him straight up,' Luke said, and saw that May had now joined them, carrying paperwork and a phone. 'Was that the mother in the ED?'

'Yes. They've had to sedate her.' May briefed him as they walked at pace through the corridors. 'They're reducing her hip in the ED.'

'What about the father?'

'He's coming from Heathrow. They'd just dropped him off there.' She grimaced.

'Can someone try and get him on the line for me? If I can get verbal consent…?'

'I've got the father on hold now—Mr Williams,' May said, but before she handed him the phone she brought him up to speed, 'Identical twins,' she informed Luke, in case he didn't already know.

'I'm aware.'

'Just check for any identifying features. Best to confirm we've got the right twin. The mother was hysterical on scene. The other little boy's still trapped.' Luke said nothing, just listened as May spoke on. 'The father's first name is Evan; the wife is Amber. Darcy's twin brother is called Hamish.'

Poor man, Luke thought, and took a steadying breath before taking the phone as he walked up to theatre.

'Mr Williams,' he said, introducing himself, but he didn't get any further.

'The police are bringing me there now. We're fifteen minutes away,' the panicked man said. 'Is there any chance I can see Darcy before you operate?'

'I'm sorry, no. I can't wait.' Luke was firm in his decision and he listed the boy's injuries. 'Every moment is vital. Now, Mr Williams, before you give your consent, we need to be as sure as we can that we have the right twin.'

Mr Williams was clearly used to the question, and as Luke put the telephone on speaker he said, 'Darcy has a strawberry birthmark behind his left ear.'

May halted the trolley and did the brief check. 'He does,' Luke said.

But after Mr Williams had given consent he started to break down. Unfortunately there wasn't even time for that.

'The anaesthetist wants to have a brief word.'

He handed the phone to the Remi, whom he'd been working with a lot these past few days. She was an elegant redhead, and she spoke calmly to the man. 'So he has asthma?' she checked and then asked if he'd ever been intubated before.

'I'm going to be with your son,' Remi assured the father. 'I'm not leaving his side.'

She was very, very kind as she told the anguished father she had a daughter the same age.

Then, 'You can tell him that yourself,' Remi said. 'He's intubated, so he can't respond, but I'll put the phone to his ear. Your daddy's on the phone, Darcy…'

Luke was so grateful for Remi. He could not bring any emotion into Theatre, and snapped his focus to the operation ahead. He always felt great responsibility when operating, but especially when it was a child. Knowing the child's father wasn't even here, Luke felt the trust placed in him fall heavy on his shoulders this morning.

Remi feels it too, Luke thought, looking thoughtful as she spoke with the rest of the theatre staff while he raced ahead to scrub in. She remained close to the little boy, stroking his hair and talking to him.

'Where's David?' he asked, when Fiona arrived alone.

'Still in Emergency,' Fiona said, and he could hear the slight trembling in her voice. 'A fourth patient was brought in. They only got notified last-minute.'

'You'll be fine,' Luke said reassuringly.

He was such a small fellow, Luke thought as Darcy was moved over. His ribs were visible. But the thing that twisted Luke was his little knees, one with a bruise and the other covered with a plaster. Though they were quickly covered by green theatre drapes, it was that brief glimpse of a normal little boy who must have recently tripped and fallen that got to Luke. And then there was the thought of a father racing across the city to get to his son...

He couldn't think of that now.

Very deliberately, he hadn't asked for any updates on the other twin. He simply wouldn't allow emotion into the operating room, but he was grateful that his anaesthetist did.

'Daddy's coming,' Remi told the boy, over and over, and, even though he was now under anaesthetic, she was still stroking the little boy's dark hair and reassuring him. 'And Mummy's here at the hospital.'

How he needed his upcoming break, Luke thought. It was getting more difficult with each passing day to push emotion aside and focus on the job.

'Let's start.' He glanced at the scrub nurse. 'Good to see you.'

They'd done a couple of cases together before, and he knew she was excellent, but apart from the brief greeting he said little. Gone were the days when he'd chatted at work, or spoken easily with the other staff.

Well, with one exception… But there was no space in his mind for anyone other than Darcy Williams right now.

'Splenectomy,' he said, as soon as the abdomen was open. What he saw confirmed his decision to remove the spleen, because it looked as if it was beyond saving, and any attempt to do so would take precious time from the other injuries. 'Perforated bowel.'

He surveyed the damage with a practised eye and was so grateful for his time in Philadelphia and the lessons passed on to him there—the main one by Carl, the chief under whom he'd worked: *'Do what you have to, then what you can…'*

Fiona did an incredible job—the whole team did.

David, his registrar, was already with his patient when Luke got to Recovery—the unexpected fourth arrival.

'Motorcyclist,' David explained. 'Looked like minor injuries at the scene but, given the mechanics of the injury, the paramedics brought him in.'

He went through the motorcyclist's injuries and the surgery that had been performed with Luke, and as David went to speak with the man's family, Luke made his way to a separate waiting room.

It was this part that he was finding increasingly difficult.

He gave it his all in Theatre, but lately, when dealing with a family, he tended to adopt a polite, professional distance, telling himself it was his surgical skills they required, not his personal ones.

Luke knocked on the closed door and went in.

Given that his wife and children had just dropped Mr Williams off at the airport, Luke had expected a businessman around his own age, in a suit, but instead an incredibly young-looking man dressed in a high-vis vest was pacing anxiously.

'Mr Williams?'

'Evan,' the man said. 'Is it bad news?'

'Darcy's in Recovery,' Luke told him straight away. 'Shall we sit?' he suggested as the young man almost dropped in relief. 'Soon we'll be moving him to the ICU.'

'Is he awake?'

'The anaesthetist did rouse him briefly at the end of his surgery, but we're going to be keeping him sedated for the next few days. However, he responded appropriately, fighting the tube and moving all his limbs. That's good news,' he added, and then carefully he went through the boy's injuries, both the good and the bad. 'He doesn't appear to have any serious head injuries,' he finished.

'He was unconscious, though. They said his heart stopped!'

'His heart didn't stop. It slowed to a dangerous level because he'd lost a lot of blood,' Luke explained. 'I had to remove his spleen.' He saw the father wince, then bury his face in his hands as Luke mentioned the bruised kidney. 'In Theatre, we found a small perforation to his bowel. It closed nicely. We've avoided a colostomy.'

Mr Williams swallowed air a few times. 'What about his legs?'

'His legs are fine.'

'Someone said…' He pressed his fingers into his eyes. 'No, I'm getting mixed up.'

'Your wife has leg injuries.'

'I know, but…'

Mr Williams was clearly overloaded with information.

'Darcy has a couple of old bruises on his knees. I saw a plaster on one,' Luke said, and watched the father's mouth stretch into a pale smile.

'He loves plasters.'

The bad news hadn't ended yet.

'Darcy's had to have a lot of blood. We're still transfusing him.' He didn't want to overwhelm the father, but the volume of the blood transfused was of great concern. 'While he desperately needs the blood, we need to monitor him very closely in case he runs into complications.' Luke decided that was enough for now. 'You should be able to see him before he's moved to the ICU.' Then he asked the question he'd been avoiding prior to operating. 'Have you heard how your other son is—Hamish?'

'He's in Intensive Care at St Bede's.'

'Okay.' Luke took that in. 'Do you know any more than that?'

'He's awake, but they're talking about sedating

him.' Urgent eyes looked to Luke. 'I don't know where I should be.'

'Would you like me to call St Bede's and find out what I can?'

'Please.' He nodded. 'I was at work…'

Luke found out that Evan was an aircraft cleaner at Heathrow and had been just starting his shift when the news had hit.

'Amber drops me off at six. We have to wake the boys…put them in the car in their pyjamas… You think you're doing the right thing… They'd have been safer in bed.'

Luke had heard similar words many times from loved ones. Had they done the right thing? He'd asked the same question of himself over and over after his mother's emotional collapse. He'd insisted his father tell her about the affair…had been so certain he was right.

It was one of the reasons he found offering personal advice to families difficult. He always second-guessed himself.

'Let me find out what I can,' he said now.

Luke headed back into Recovery and checked in on the little boy, and from there he called St Bede's to find out what he could about his brother.

He was quickly transferred to the ICU.

'Sister Adams.'

'Shona.' Luke was too tired to care who it was on the other end of the line. 'I'm calling about Hamish Williams.'

'You've got his brother, I hear?'

'Correct,' Luke said. 'He's about to be moved to the ICU.' He went through the injuries and prognosis. 'Still too early to say—he's had a lot of blood.'

'DIC?' Shona asked, knowing that there could be serious issues with coagulation.

'I hope not,' Luke said. 'How's Hamish doing?'

'The main injury is a small subdural haematoma,' Shona informed him. That was a small bleed into Hamish's brain. 'He's conscious, but restless. They're talking about sedating him. Horace is with him now. I can get him to speak with you?'

'Don't pull him away,' Luke said, pleased that Hamish was under the care of such a brilliant neurosurgeon. 'I really just want to know what to tell the father. If he's needed more here or there.'

'Give me a moment. I'll see what I can find out.'

'Thanks.'

It was a long moment.

Luke didn't like Shona. In fact, he actively disliked her. But he knew she was good at her job, and very thorough, and would be speaking with Horace now. Professionally speaking, he trusted her.

He could hear the sounds of the ICU at St Bede's, and familiar voices in the background. It felt odd to be miles away...

Shona returned to the phone. 'I've spoken to Horace. He thinks having Dad here might help settle Hamish, and at least he can be there as they sedate him.'

'Thanks,' Luke said. 'I'll let the father know.'

Without further ceremony he ended the call and headed back to Mr Williams.

'Okay.' Luke stayed standing while talking this time. 'I've spoken with St Bede's and I think it would be a great comfort to Hamish for him to have you there.'

'I see.'

It was clear Evan Williams was torn. 'The staff here will call you if there is any change, but for now Darcy's as stable as he can be.'

'So you think I should head there?'

'I do,' Luke said, knowing there was no easy answer. 'See Darcy before you leave, but then head over.'

'What about Amber? If she's awake she'll be frantic.'

'I'll go down there now and talk to her if I can. Or let the ED staff know what's happening so they can inform her when she's awake.' It did sound as if St Bede's really did want the father there. 'You go and be with Hamish.'

As the theatre nurse led Mr Williams in to see his son, Luke made his way to Emergency and updated Mrs Williams, who was awake but said little. Her face was pale with shock and pain, and she was clearly terrified for her sons. 'I need to see them.'

'I know,' Luke said. But she was about to go to theatre to have her lower leg pinned. 'It's simply not possible yet. Evan will soon be with Hamish, and Darcy is sedated.'

He came away from the grim conversation and saw the flushed face of May.

'There's a debriefing for all the personnel involved in the RTA at two.'

'I'll hopefully be asleep by then.'

'There's another one at eight for the night staff.'

'And I'll hopefully *still* be asleep then,' Luke responded.

But May tutted. 'You ought to go.'

'Are you going?'

'I have a deaf husband,' May chuckled. 'He knows when to nod and when to shake his head.'

Luke smiled, and then headed up to deal with the patients he'd been about to see before his pager had gone off, who were no doubt still waiting for him.

Luke's patients were indeed waiting for him, but Pippa knew he would come when he could.

'Where *is* Mr Harris?'

Mrs James was up at the nurses' station and agitated. She'd been hoping to take Chloe home, but there had been no early-morning ward round.

'He's still in Theatre,' Jenny said. 'It might be a while.'

'You said that two hours ago. How much longer is he going to be?'

Jenny shrugged and walked off, and although Mrs James was being prickly, Pippa knew it wasn't without reason. She was exhausted, Pippa could see that, and on top of a sick child she had a new baby at home and other concerns too—such as how she

was going to manage her usually active and demanding daughter, who really needed to have a
very quiet few weeks.

'There were several emergencies brought in this
morning,' Pippa explained.

She knew about the multi-trauma not only from
being with Luke when he was paged, but because it
had been on the news during her break. She didn't
go into any sort of detail with Mrs James, though,
just explained things as best she could.

'The operating theatres are really busy. I know
it's frustrating, but emergencies have to come first.'

'I know they do.' Mrs James closed her eyes.
'They were talking about taking Chloe to Theatre
at one point.'

While Mrs James clearly irked Jenny, she didn't
bother Pippa. In fact, she thought it nice that the
woman was so worried about her daughter and her
little baby, and how to juggle her young family.

Had it been the same for her own mother when
she'd been born?

Pippa had spent a lot of time at her aunt's house…
A lot.

She knew how delays and emergencies upended
so many things in a hospital, and even if it was true
that emergencies had to take priority, it still caused
inconvenience and upset.

'He's not going to recognise me,' Mrs James said
with a sigh.

'George?' Pippa checked, referring to Chloe's
new brother.

'I wanted to breastfeed, but that's starting to fall by the wayside.'

'Whether it's today or in a couple of days' time, you'll soon be home,' Pippa said.

But she knew getting Chloe discharged from hospital wasn't the only problem Mrs James faced.

'How am I going to keep her amused? I know she's a bit spoilt, but we thought we were just having the one child. She's already a bit jealous of the new baby.'

'I'll get the doctor to speak to her, and I'll talk to her too.' Pippa paused when she saw Luke and Fiona arriving. 'Here he is now.'

As Mrs James went to sit with her daughter, Luke and Fiona came to the desk. They both looked pretty grim—understandably so, given they had been on call all night and then operating this morning. With the added emergencies they must be dead on their feet.

'How's the child from this morning?' Pippa asked him.

'On the ICU,' Luke said, but didn't elaborate. Instead, he looked over to Fiona, who looked as white as he looked grey. 'Why don't you go and grab some lunch?' he suggested. 'And could you get me something to eat and a coffee?'

'I was going to go to the…' She paused. 'Sure.'

Fiona walked off, no doubt exhausted, and it was then that Luke pulled a face.

'Damn, she probably wants to go to the debriefing.' He brought his attention back to his patients. 'What do you have for me?'

'Just the one. Chloe James.'

'How's she been?'

'Bored. Mum's worried about her following directions at home.' Pippa smiled at Jenny as she came over with a drug sheet for Luke to sign. 'We're just about to go and see Chloe.'

'Well, remind her mum she's not the only one on the ward,' Jenny said. 'And that it's the NHS. We don't have private chefs!'

Luke didn't know exactly what Jenny meant, but guessed that Chloe wasn't happy with the food. He'd expected, perhaps, for Pippa to roll her eyes, for her to ignore Jenny's statement and simply get on, but instead Pippa turned around and looked straight at her colleague.

'Give her a break,' Pippa told Jenny.

Jenny said nothing, just took the chart, and then they went in to see Chloe.

'Take your earmuffs off, Chloe,' Mrs James said as they walked in to the small side ward.

'Sorry for the delay,' he said.

'Where have you been?' whined Chloe.

'Busy,' Luke said. 'How are you?'

'Better!' Chloe said. 'I want to go home.'

'Then let me take a look at you. You've been eating?'

'I had a takeaway last night.'

Luke turned sharply to Pippa. 'I specifically instructed that she was to be on a low-fat diet.'

'She didn't like the dinner,' Mrs James hurriedly explained.

But Luke shook his head. 'I don't want her eating takeaway. Not until she's been seen in Outpatients.'

'But we're getting pizza tonight,' Chloe protested.

'Do you want to go home?' he asked.

'Yes.'

'Okay, then let's take a look at you.'

Having examined her, he sat on the chair by her bed. Pippa could almost feel his weariness, but he smiled at the little girl and her mother.

'Chloe will need to come in to the clinic in two weeks' time.'

'Can she go to school next week?'

'No school until we see her at the clinic, and then it will be a modified return.'

'What does "modified" mean?' Chloe asked.

'No sport for a while,' Luke said.

Now might not be the right time to tell her she wouldn't be able to go out at playtime for a little while yet, so he qualified his words.

'Or anything like that. We'll talk about it at your Outpatients appointment. I need to have a private word with your mother, but first I want you to listen to me. You are going to have to do everything your mother says for the next few weeks and eat what she gives you. No takeaway, no pizza. Just plain food.'

She pulled a face.

'It's very important, Chloe. If you don't, I'll find

out at the clinic and tell your mum that there's to be no Disney.'

'No!'

'Yes,' he said. 'That injury in your tummy is getting better every day, but I don't want you falling or getting knocked over and having to come back here. This is very important.'

'Okay…'

'You've had a nasty knock and I don't want you climbing or playing roughly with anyone for a while. No jumping up and down on the bed or the sofa. You might be bored, but you can manage that for a couple of weeks, can't you?'

Chloe gave a reluctant nod.

'I'll see you in the clinic, then, unless I hear from your mother before.'

He hoped he was stern, but kind, and knew the clinic appointment in two weeks would take a lot of pressure off Chloe's exhausted mother.

He spoke to Mrs James outside the ward and told her to use his name as a threat as much as she liked. 'If she wants to play, or eat something unsuitable, tell her you're going to call me, or that you already have and that I've said no. Mrs James, this isn't a punishment. This is about her recovery from a serious injury.'

'Yes, I understand.' She closed her eyes. 'Thank you for everything.'

'My pleasure. I'll see both in two weeks. Take very good care.'

They shook hands, but before Pippa could follow Mrs James back into the side ward, he looked over to her.

'Nurse, can I have a quick word?'

'Sure.' She smiled at Mrs James. 'I'll be in with you in a moment.'

Pippa and Luke stood by the linen trolley, which was hardly private, but it would look as if they were just discussing work.

'Thanks for the coffee, earlier,' he said.

'My pleasure,' she said, and smiled begrudgingly. 'Sort of.'

'Well, it was much appreciated.'

'It sounds as if it was pretty grim…'

'Yep. Poor kid. He had this plaster on his knee…'

And even though he halted, Pippa understood exactly what he meant.

'It's the little things,' she ventured. 'They get to you sometimes.'

Luke said nothing, but he gave a small, weary nod.

He looked at her then. 'It seems a long time since that night.'

Pippa gave a soft, slightly ironic laugh. It felt like an *eternity*, and while she knew he'd been impossibly busy, they'd parted without any promises or plans and she hated the uncertainty.

'I think tonight's a write-off,' Luke said. 'I'll see, but…'

He'd see?

Had he not been so obviously dead on his feet,

Pippa would have shot back a smart retort. Thankfully, he was saved from seeing her pursed lips, because Fiona returned, with a paper bag containing food and a large coffee for her boss.

'Thanks.'

'Do you want me to go to Surg One?' Fiona offered. 'Start the paperwork on the discharges?'

'No,' he said, shaking his head. 'I'll do it. You head off to the debriefing.'

'What about you?'

'I don't need a debrief. I didn't work on the fatality.' Luke shrugged. 'I'll see you tomorrow, Fiona. Thanks for your help—especially in Theatre this morning. You did an incredible job. It was touch and go for a while.'

Pippa had watched the exchange, and as Fiona walked off she saw him pull a face as he opened up the bag and pulled out a Scotch egg and a bag of crisps.

'And I tell the patients not to eat junk!'

'Do as say, not as I do.' Pippa smiled, but it wavered. She could see his mind was elsewhere. 'Nola said there were young twins involved,' Pippa ventured. 'Have you heard how the other one is?'

'I've been focussing on the patient I had.' Luke's response was a touch curt, but then he seemed to check himself. 'The other twin has a head injury. His father's in a taxi on his way to him at St Bede's now. I believe the mother's on her way to Theatre.'

'Gosh...'

'Hopefully they're all going to make a full recovery.' He took a bite of Scotch egg. 'Unlike my arteries.'

'You prefer health food?'

'Not really. I just prefer my eggs not to be wrapped in sausage meat and deep-fried!' He shook his head, and then managed a half-wave as he went to walk off. 'Ignore me. It's been a long night...'

Luke couldn't ignore his thoughts of Pippa, though.

He woke late in the evening in a bed that held the subtle scent of summer on a dark wintery evening. He thought about calling her, but knew he wouldn't be great company tonight.

Instead, he returned a call from his father.

'You called?' Luke said curtly, because when his mother wasn't around they were still barely talking.

'Good to hear from you,' Matthew Harris said, in the cheery voice that indicated he was at home. 'Your mother wants to talk about our fortieth anniversary.'

'You're not serious,' Luke replied.

'I know it's a way off,' Matthew carried on cheerfully, as if his son wasn't sending daggers down the phone, 'but we want you to pencil in the date. Hold on a moment...'

Luke lay there, looking at a ceiling that needed painting.

'Your mother wants to know when you're coming over.'

'I'll call her,' Luke said. 'It's pretty full on at The Primary.'

'Well, you insisted on crossing to the other side,' his father quipped. 'I heard you got the brunt of that multi-trauma.'

'Yep.'

'We had a couple admitted...'

Luke said nothing in response. He didn't want updates—especially if the news wasn't good.

His father broke the silence. 'So, what are you up to?'

'I'm about to have something to eat and then go back to sleep. I'm back on tomorrow at seven.'

'Come over,' Matthew suggested.

'And go through the guest list for your party?' Luke asked, with more than an edge to his tone, because he knew his mother would insist on his father's colleagues being invited. Who knew whether his latest mistress would be amongst them? 'I don't think so.'

'I meant,' Matthew said, 'come and have some supper. Your mother's about to go into her studio to paint. We can talk...'

'I thought you didn't want to discuss things.'

'I meant come over and get the hospital out of your head for a bit. You know what they say—all work and no play...'

'Don't,' Luke warned, because he did not need one of his father's little pep talks.

And yet behind the jovial tone he knew that, despite appearances, certain patients did get to his father and he was trying to connect. Luke just didn't want to hear it tonight.

'I'm going back to sleep. Tell Mum I'll call her soon.'

Luke ended the call and tossed the phone onto the mattress. He was still furious with his father—he simply did not get why a man who had everything would risk it all.

No, he didn't get it.

He tried to get back to sleep, but the scent of summer was still on his pillow and in this instance his father was right. All work and no play did make one dull, Luke thought, and came up with his usual solution as he pulled up Pippa's number. He wanted food, and sex, though when he thought of the night they had spent together, possibly not in that order...

'Hey,' he said when she answered. 'I just woke up.' He glanced at the time and saw that it was almost nine. 'I know it's a bit late.'

'It's fine,' Pippa said, though he could barely hear her. 'What do you want?'

'You,' Luke said, because usually it was that easy. 'And food.'

'Then you'd better get dressed.'

Only then did he hear the music in the background. 'Where are you?'

'Thanks, Rohan.' Pippa took two paper plates piled with scented dahl and roti bread and handed one to her late guest.

It was all very well being bright and spontaneous, but Pippa knew boundaries were urgently required if she was to hold on to her heart.

Determined not to be sitting at home if he called, Pippa had made herself go out. As Rohan had said, the Diwali atmosphere was incredible, and whether or not Luke called, Pippa was glad to have come out and seen it.

'You two know each other?' Luke checked as they walked to the river's edge, because he'd seen Pippa had bypassed quite a queue to get their food.

'Rohan works at the coffee shop I use,' she explained. 'That's his father's truck.'

They stood, looking at the London Eye, all lit up in a rainbow of colours that meant good luck and prosperity. They dipped hot roti into fragrant dahl, but all too soon his bread was gone.

Pippa still had a decent bit left, and he eyed it hungrily. 'I'm starving, Pippa...'

'Then line up,' she said, and popped the last piece of roti in her mouth.

They dropped their plates into a bin and then got back to enjoying the music and the lights.

'Any interest in the apartment?' she asked.

'No idea,' Luke said. 'Given that I'd hoped to be in bed, I told them no viewings today. How was your day?'

'It was all right,' Pippa said, even though for the most part it had been difficult. But she was determined not to get into all that.

And this was why, she told herself. Because with his arm around her, watching the lanterns bobbing on the Thames, she was as happy as she knew how to be.

She'd lit one for Julia, before Luke had arrived.

Not that she'd tell him that.

But now she stared at the lights and knew that hers was out there.

'You're freezing,' he said, and turned her to face him.

'I've been here since sunset.' She thought for a moment. 'Luke, I know what you said the other day, but I don't want anyone at work knowing about...' she gave a casual shrug '...this.'

'They won't hear it from me.'

'Good.'

'You don't want them knowing about your wild side?' he asked.

'Something like that,' Pippa said, and then she told him what she'd decided. 'But don't think I'm on call for you, Luke. I won't be waiting by the phone, and nor will I be at your beck and call.'

Luke turned her to face him and looked at her properly. She looked far from wild.

Pippa wore a grey woolly hat, and the curls escaping it were soft from the damp air. Her scarf was double-wrapped, and he ached to unravel it and expose her pale neck. But there would be time for that later.

Right now, it was nice to take in the night and this woman who had dragged him from his bed to civilisation.

The lights from the river and above their heads were reflected in her pale cheeks, and the wind was making her eyes glassy. And, while he would have liked to still those chattering lips with a kiss, instead he took her frozen hands and placed then beneath his coat and pulled her in.

'You're right,' he agreed. 'And I wouldn't expect you to be on call for me,' he said.

He had enjoyed getting out this evening, slightly to his surprise, and it also occurred to him that it felt good to be back in London…

Pippa closed her eyes and held on to his warmth. When she opened them, she saw all the lanterns and smiled. She felt like an imposter in the body of a woman who knew how to let loose and be happy…

She rested her head on his chest, hearing the thump-thump of his heart and blinking back sudden tears as she saw the lanterns floating out of view.

She never cried.

She definitely wasn't about to start now.

Thankfully, he made her smile instead.

'The heating is on at mine,' he said into the shell of her pale, cold ear. 'Come on,' he told her, taking her hand and leading her through the happy crowds.

But Pippa halted him.

'Do you have milk?'

'We can get some on the way.'

He didn't call it home.

Yet.

Ah, but London had her ways…

CHAPTER SEVEN

THEY WERE GOING to be late.

'Go!' Pippa said as she came out of the shower, watching as Luke hastily attempted to make the bed. 'I'll do it. You have to be at work by seven.'

'I do,' he agreed, selecting a tie from his wardrobe and putting up his shirt collar. 'So hurry up and get dressed.'

Pippa shook her head. 'I can take the Tube. I don't have to be there until half-past.'

'Or is it that you don't want to be seen arriving with me.'

'Both,' Pippa openly agreed.

Only her words clearly didn't offend him, because rather than picking up his keys and heading out he crossed the bedroom towards her.

It had been a week since that night at The Avery.

And even without her contacts in Luke in the morning was a very nice sight indeed.

'You haven't shaved,' Pippa said, not because he was close enough for her to see it, but because his farewell kiss was rough and probing and his hand was moving to the knot on her towel.

'When is there time to shave?'

'Go!' Pippa said, even though she'd rather not be the sensible one.

'You're bad for me, Pippa,' he said, reluctantly releasing her.

'I think it's the other way round!' Pippa joked as he walked out through the door.

Or rather, he was by far too good for her, Pippa thought as she heard his footsteps fade on the stairs.

She didn't mean that he was too good for her in a self-deprecating way—more that this week had been the best she'd ever known.

And not just making love—though there had been plenty of that in their busy schedules. As well as the evening they spent at the Diwali celebrations, they'd crammed in a candlelit concert in a gorgeous cathedral, and just last night, though she'd been on a late shift, they'd taken his neighbour's puppy for a walk.

'How did we get roped into this?' Luke had asked as the puppy had sat and refused either to wee or walk. 'It's your fault!'

Pippa had not been able to resist patting Sausage one day in the corridor, and the next thing they knew Luke had been lumbered with feeding it and walking it.

Finally the puppy had weed, and he'd picked it up and carried it home. Then they'd let the puppy back into its owner's apartment.

'"It's just this once",' Pippa had said, mimicking the owner's voice, as they'd given Sausage his necessary treats and then placed him in his crate. 'Mind you,' she'd added as they'd left, 'that's how it starts…'

'And that's how it ends,' Luke had said, posting

the keys through the letterbox, clearly refusing to get embroiled.

He had said he didn't like to get involved, and if she'd needed any further proof then this was it.

Now, instead of making the bed, Pippa sat on it. She kept a strip of contact lenses at his flat now, and she popped a fresh pair in. The room certainly looked clearer, and her eyes landed on a couple of packing boxes neatly stacked in the corner, under the large, ugly painting the estate agent had chosen to draw attention away from the bumpy wall.

The bedroom felt silent without their easy chatter—yes, easy, because they didn't really touch on anything deep. Luke refused to bring his work home with him, and neither of them spoke much about family. Occasionally they touched on the past—a teacher they'd both had, or a person they recalled—but nothing too weighty.

And, given they weren't looking to the future, she didn't tell him of her surprise that she'd been called back for a second interview; nor did he mention his upcoming job in Scotland or whatever lay beyond that.

They were happily suspended in the now.

But in the peace and quiet of the morning there was too much space for the thoughts that Pippa had been trying to ignore.

In a couple of weeks Luke would be gone.

You got through it once before, Pippa reminded herself.

Yet she'd been sixteen then, and hadn't known his kiss, let alone anything else.

Now she knew how it felt to touch him, to have him on her and in her... How behind that rather brusque demeanour he was still the guy she'd met that day in the library...

He still had a piece of her heart, and Pippa was doing all she could not to let it show.

'We're expecting an admission from the ICU,' the night sister informed the day staff. 'Darcy Williams, five years old.'

'From the multi-trauma?' Pippa checked.

She nodded. 'Splenectomy, contusion on left kidney, perforated bowel and concussion. He was extubated forty-eight hours ago. GCS thirteen to fifteen.'

The Glasgow Coma Scale was a score given to measure the severity or worsening of a brain injury, and fifteen was the best score, so Darcy was doing well.

'He's opening his eyes, though mainly to verbal command, but he's barely talking. His mother was admitted here, but she's being discharged today. His identical twin was taken to another trauma centre.'

'What about the father?'

'Running in between hospitals, apparently.'

'When should we expect Darcy?'

'I've told them we won't have a side room until lunchtime.' Laura raised her hands skywards. 'But they want to send him up before that.'

'Just tell them we're not ready,' a grumpy Jenny snapped, but thankfully Nola stepped in.

'Pippa, can you see about moving Room Four up to the main ward? She's due for discharge.'

It became a dance of the beds, because Mrs Williams had a serious leg injury, and Room Four was the smallest, so it would be difficult for her to move around in there alongside her son's bed when she visited. But finally Room Seven was ready and waiting, meds and breakfasts had been given, and Jenny was feeding Toby at the desk because his parents weren't in yet.

'Hi, Luke,' Nola said as he came up to the desk.

'Is my admission here?' he asked.

'Not yet.' Nola called over to Pippa. 'Go and have your break before he gets here.'

'Sure…'

As Luke went to check on his other patients Pippa made a mug of—horrible—coffee and found Fiona sitting in the break room.

'Is Darcy here?' she asked. 'The ICU admission?'

'Not yet.' Pippa shook her head. 'They'll buzz if he arrives—that's why I'm on my break.'

It was actually a relief to be away from the ward while Luke was on it. Pippa still felt a blush creeping up when he was around, and he wasn't quite as discreet as her. He often pulled her aside, more than willing to chat or even discuss their evening plans, when Pippa would have preferred things to stay strictly professional at work and to be kept private between them.

'Have you heard how the other twin is?' Pippa asked.

'He's doing well.' Fiona nodded. 'They're talking about moving him to the neuro ward. I've asked Luke about transferring him here.'

'And?'

'He says it's not my decision,' Fiona responded tartly. 'Easy enough for him to say when he's not the one dealing with the parents.'

Pippa said nothing.

'He's brilliant in Theatre,' Fiona elaborated to her silent audience. 'And I know you have to have a certain ruthlessness to do his job. But still, a little sensitivity outside the operating room wouldn't go amiss.'

Still Pippa said nothing. Okay, Luke wasn't all jokes and small talk—and, yes, he was strict with his orders. But it was always with the patient's best interests in mind.

Still, Fiona hadn't quite finished, and now she was giving a dramatic eyeroll. 'He's always been like that…'

'Like what?'

'Straight on to the next one…' She raised her eyebrows meaningfully. 'And not just with his patients.'

Pippa left Fiona to it and returned from her break early. Darcy still hadn't arrived, and Luke was looking at X-rays, his phone tucked into his neck. He was sounding less than impressed.

'Seriously?' Luke's voice was impatient as he spoke into the phone. 'How am I supposed to manage that when I have ward rounds at seven?' He shook his head impatiently. 'Let me get back to you…'

'Trouble?' Nola asked.

'Apparently so.' He sighed, pocketing his phone, and then, perhaps seeing Pippa appear, he asked Nola, 'Do you make your bed in the morning?'

'Of course,' Nola said.

'Jenny?'

'I was in the army,' Jenny answered. 'So yes.'

'And do you tidy the bathroom? Wipe down the shower?'

She nodded.

Then he glanced over at Pippa, who must surely have gone as red as a beetroot.

'Pippa,' he asked, 'do you make your bed in the morning?'

'Of course,' she croaked, knowing full well what he was referring to. Not only had she not made the bed this morning, she'd dressed in a hurry and left his bathroom in morning chaos.

'*Every* morning?' he checked, and she looked up to see his incredulous smile.

'If I'm on night duty, yes,' Pippa amended. 'If I'm on a late, sometimes…'

'What about if you're on an early?'

'That depends.' Pippa shook her head and refused to flirt, but both of them knew they were discussing this morning.

'Well, I've just been told by my estate agent that if I want people brought round while I'm at work I'm to leave my flat inspection-ready.'

'Obviously,' Jenny said.

'I got the golden package. I thought they'd at least—'

'You thought the estate agent would dash around and do a quick tidy?' Jenny harumphed as she walked off. 'Oh, no…'

Luke waited till Pippa was in the drug room and then wagged a finger as he walked in. 'What happened to "I'll do it"?' he quoted back her own words.

'I lost track of time,' Pippa admitted, but instead of telling him she'd been sitting on the bed, thinking how impossible it would be to say goodbye to him, she came up with something lighter. 'I was looking at your walls.'

'My walls?'

'Yes, they need wallpaper. But if you don't have time for that then, like I said, you should dress up the fireplaces rather than put ugly prints on the wall.'

'Says the would-be interior designer? I'll leave it to the experts, thanks.'

'It's okay, Luke,' Pippa said with a smirk, seeing his slight look of horror, as if his latest squeeze had told her she was thinking of moving in. 'I'm not hoping for a trip to IKEA with you, or to pick out bedspreads. I just love old buildings.'

'Luke,' Jenny called. 'Your ICU transfer's here.'

'Thanks.'

Pippa went too, as she had been assigned to care for little Darcy. His father was with him, and he and Luke were clearly on first-name terms.

'Hi, Evan,' Luke said, and then went over to his little patient. 'Hey, Darcy. You're looking even better than you did this morning.'

Dark, solemn grey eyes looked briefly at Luke and then flicked away.

He was recovering well from his dreadful injuries, Pippa heard from the ICU nurse who gave hand-over.

'Luke has said he can start on sips of water, but so far he's refusing. He's really quiet, which is apparently unusual for him. He's barely spoken, except a couple of times to ask for his mum.'

'She's being discharged this morning?' Pippa checked.

'Yes. You know he has an identical twin?'

'I do.'

'They're arranging transport so Mum can visit Hamish, then she'll come here. Darcy hasn't asked for his brother or anything, which Dad says is also unusual. He's really withdrawn.'

Evan, the twins' father, walked over then, and thanked the ICU nurse for her care. When she'd left he spoke to Pippa.

'My wife and I are going to take it in turns to stay with Darcy, but Amber's got a fractured leg.'

'Yes, we've put Darcy in the biggest side room, so that we can put a recliner in there for her, as well as a bed.' She glanced into the side room and saw the anaesthetist had also arrived to assess Darcy, and there was quite a crowd in there now. 'I'll show you the facilities.'

'Thanks.'

Pippa took Evan round and showed him the parents' room and the small kitchenette, as well as the shower and bathroom. 'How's Hamish doing?' she asked.

'Better than Darcy,' Evan said with a relieved sigh. 'He's off the ventilator and talking. A little bit confused... I'm crossing my fingers that he can be transferred here. I've asked Mr Harris if he can look into it, but I haven't heard yet whether it's possible...'

Darcy was indeed very subdued, his eyes barely tracking as Pippa did his obs late that afternoon, though he did look up when Luke came into the room.

'How are you feeling, Darcy?'

He didn't answer, just turned his head away.

'Who's this?' Pippa asked, tickling the face of the scruffy and clearly much-loved teddy Darcy had tucked under his arm.

'That's Whiskers.' Evan spoke for his silent son.

'Does Hamish have a bear?' Pippa asked as she

checked the various drips. Out of the corner of her eye she saw Darcy stir.

'Coco,' Darcy whispered.

'And is Coco with Hamish now?' Pippa asked.

And even though it was Evan who answered, he was clearly pleased at the one-word response from his son.

'Yes. Amber told me to fetch them the day after the accident. The boys hide them when their friends come to play.'

'You hide them?' Pippa gave Darcy a shocked look, then smiled at the little boy. 'I hide my teddy too. Mind you, I'm a lot older than you...'

But Darcy wasn't engaging any longer. He just closed his eyes and held on to his bear and lay there listlessly as he was examined.

'Try and get him to take some fluids,' Luke told Evan, moving away from the bedside.

'He's not really interested.'

'The drip is keeping him hydrated,' Luke explained, 'but if you can encourage him to drink it will aid his recovery.'

Soon it became a bit of an issue.

Unlike little Chloe, who had been begging to drink and to eat, Darcy continued to show no interest in food or fluids.

'He wants his brother,' Nola said to Luke late the next afternoon. 'Can't you speak to Allocations?'

'It has nothing to do with Allocations,' Luke responded tartly. 'His brother is on a top neuro ward and really wouldn't benefit from an ambulance ride across town.' He glanced over as Jenny called his name. 'Yes?'

'Martha wants to speak with you,' she said, gesturing with her head towards the office.

'Sure.'

But as he stood Evan Williams made his way over to ask again if there was any chance of his other son being transferred.

'It would just make things easier all around,' the harried father said. 'And I know it would cheer Darcy up.'

'I do understand where you're coming from,' Luke said.

Pippa was feeding a baby at the desk, so she was able to listen as he explained the situation a little more gently to the father.

'By all accounts Hamish is doing well, but he's had a serious bleed on the brain and he needs to be closely monitored. I don't think a transfer right now is in his best interests. He's where he needs to be.'

'I know he is…' Evan ran a tired hand over his forehead. 'Darcy wants me to take Hamish his bear. I told Darcy he needs it for now, and that Hamish has Coco with him.'

'Probably wise,' Luke said.

No! Pippa glanced up, wanting to intervene. If Darcy wanted Hamish to have *his* bear, then that was probably the right thing.

But Nola was in on the conversation now, and was agreeing with both Luke and Evan. As well as that, the social worker had arrived and Martha, the paediatrician, was at the desk. It wasn't Pippa's place, especially in front of Mr Williams, to disagree.

As they all moved into the NUM's office to discuss things, Pippa not only wanted the PAC Unit job more than ever, she knew she was right for it. Knew she was ready to have more of a voice.

'Luke?' she said as soon as he stepped out of the meeting.

'What?' He was tense and distracted. 'I'm waiting for a consult from Mr Benson. Can you fetch me the moment he calls?'

'Sure,' Pippa said.

'In the meantime, ask Toby's parents to come through to the NUM's office.'

Pippa nodded, but she was frowning, because Toby wasn't his patient.

Then she saw Jenny, standing by the cot, making small talk with the parents—which was unusual for Jenny. It was clear to Pippa that she wasn't letting the baby out of her sight.

Nola came out then, and briefly brought Pippa up to speed: some rather worrying information had come to light regarding Toby.

The social worker wasn't here about Darcy and Hamish, Pippa realised. The moment to talk about teddies and on whose bed they belonged had passed.

CHAPTER EIGHT

EVEN BEFORE SIX in the morning it was already her happiest birthday ever.

Although Luke didn't know that he'd just made love to a thirty-year-old!

Pippa lay facing the wall, with Luke spooning her, both relishing the aftershocks of early-morning sex. The alarm hadn't even gone off yet.

'Sorry to wake you,' he said.

'You can wake me like that every morning!'

Pippa smiled to herself, but it soon faded as she realised there wouldn't be many more mornings like this.

Still, if this was how it felt to be thirty, Pippa thought, then bring it on!

She hadn't told Luke that today was her birthday, and it wasn't just because they were keeping things light. She never made a big deal out of it.

Nor did her parents.

There would be a card with some cash in it waiting for her the next time she called in. Still, given it was a milestone birthday perhaps she hoped they might call and ask her to come over. Surprise her with cake...

Pippa was aware that birthdays were extremely painful for them. Her own eighteenth and twenty-first had barely been mentioned, and on what would have been Julia's thirtieth, her mother had been in bits.

Pippa closed her eyes, trying not to recall the tears and drama and return to the blissful floaty feeling of being wrapped in Luke's arms, feeling safe and warm on a cold late-November day.

Even the alarm didn't intrude on the pleasure, because Luke uncoiled himself from her and turned it off. Instead of rolling straight out of bed, as was his usual practice, he turned on her electric blanket topper, turned onto his back and pulled her into him.

'There is an advantage to staying at yours…' he said.

'Because we don't have to make the bed and tidy up?'

'Well, there's that,' he agreed. 'I meant it's closer to work. We don't have to rush.'

'True.'

There was even time for tea and toast, topped with ginger marmalade from the night market they'd been to earlier in the week. It was fiery and spicy and the perfect winter breakfast.

They were now both 'two toothbrush households'—something he'd said drily when, having first ended up back at hers, morning had broken and there'd been no time for him to go home and wash and change before work. Thankfully, Pippa had found him a spare toothbrush, and now he brushed his teeth at her place with a neon pink one. At his, Pippa had the spare toothbrush from the goody-bag from his flight home from the States.

They weren't yet 'two deodorant households'. So it was Luke's turn to smell of baby powder for the day. Fair enough, given that for most of this week Pippa's usual scent of summer had been rather drowned out by some kind of twenty-four-hour-lasting concoction for 'active men'.

Luke even had a couple of shirts hanging in her wardrobe, still in their plastic from the dry-cleaning service, and as he ripped open one of the covers, Luke couldn't help but think how he usually used the lack of a fresh shirt or a toothbrush or whatever as a good reason to head off early, or even leave in the middle of the night.

Not now.

When Pippa had said she needed to pick up her dry-cleaning, it had prompted him to throw a few clean shirts into the car.

It just made things easier.

Or rather, it made things a little more compli-cated than he was used to... But then, he reasoned, their affair would be so short-lived that it wouldn't matter. It was good to spend as much time as they had together rather than shuffling back and forth.

He looked at Pippa, lying in bed watching him and wearing a sleepy smile.

'The blanket's warming up,' she said, with all the temptation of a practised seductress.

'That's not fair,' he said, knowing she was naked and warm beneath the sheets. For the first time ever he was considering being late for rounds. 'Have you got your contacts in?'

'No.' She smiled.

'Pity…'

'I'm not blind!' Pippa laughed, and looked down at how turned on he was, and then back up to his face. 'You know you want to…'

He resisted temptation—but with a proviso. 'I should be able to get off at a reasonable time tonight,' he said. 'Maybe we could—'

'I'm not sure I can tonight,' Pippa interrupted. 'I'll let you know.'

'I'm on call tomorrow night,' he reminded her.

It wasn't like Luke to push, but he was getting to the pointy end of his contract and time was fading fast. He'd also had to put a deposit down for a cottage he'd found…

'I've found a nice place in Scotland… Skye,' he told her. 'A stone cottage, with peat fires in both the bedroom and lounge.'

'Estate-agent-speak for freezing,' Pippa said with authority. 'Does it have hot water?'

'I assume so.'

'Never assume.'

'You can take a look tonight,' Luke said.

And then he halted—not just because she'd said she might have plans, but because in recent days he'd been thinking of asking if she would join him for a couple of weeks in Scotland. He'd never done anything like that with another woman.

'Or whenever,' he amended, pulling on his suit jacket and trying to quash the thought of spoiling things by suggesting they extend their arrangement.

'You can make sure I won't be fetching my water from a well…'

Pippa gave him a thin smile, deciding she definitely would *not* be helping him choose the accommodation that would be enjoyed by his next lover…

When he'd left, she checked her phone, hoping for a birthday message—then reminded herself it wasn't even seven yet. Her parents would barely be awake.

They still hadn't messaged when Pippa checked her phone later that morning, when she was on her break.

She didn't get to go to lunch until late, because Darcy threw up in a major way. Evan had gone with Amber to visit Hamish, and Darcy was teary, so Pippa changed his bedding while Laura went to page Fiona to come and check on him.

'It's okay, Darcy,' Pippa told him, when he was tucked up in a clean bed with his teddy. 'Mummy will be back soon.'

'I'll stay with him,' Laura said, coming back into the room. 'Fiona's going to come when she can.'

Eating her cheese sandwich, Pippa went through her messages, but although a couple of friends had texted, as well as her aunt, there was nothing from her parents.

Pippa was more angry than hurt.

Or was she more hurt than angry?

She honestly didn't know how she felt as she headed back to the ward.

Evan was back from visiting his other son, but Amber was staying with Hamish for now.

Fiona had come to see Darcy.

'How's that tummy?' she asked as she gently probed Darcy's stomach.

But Darcy didn't answer her. Instead, he looked over to the more familiar face of Pippa. 'Where's Hamish?'

'He's being looked after in another hospital,' Pippa told the little boy, as she had many times before. 'Darcy, the doctor wants to know if your tummy's sore.'

Darcy just turned his little head and carried on staring out at the grey afternoon.

'Is he drinking anything?' asked Fiona.

'Just small sips,' Pippa said, 'and only with a lot of encouragement.'

'So just the one vomit?' Fiona checked, and Pippa nodded. 'I might speak to David…'

'Thanks.'

It was Luke who came to check on the patient later in the afternoon, but there were no clinical changes.

'I'm going to call the anaesthetist and ask her to come and do a pain review,' he told Pippa. 'And I'll increase his IV fluids. He's very listless.'

Luke was more than aware that he was the bad guy here. Especially as there was an empty twin-bedded room that had opened up on the paediatric ward.

Darcy wanted his twin!

As he sat at the desk checking labs, Nola pointed it out to him.

'So I've repeatedly been told,' Luke snapped.

By several of the staff, by the bed allocations team, and by Darcy's father, who had just brought Amber back to be with Darcy and was now peering into the spare two-bed room…

Luke was well aware of the impact on the family, and had even touched on the prospect of a transfer with Horace. For now, though, both had chosen to err on the side of caution and agreed that, for the time being, it was better that each twin stay where he was.

'Delivery for Pippa Westford.'

Luke glanced up at the delivery man and saw a huge potted plant that surely belonged in some retro musical land on the edge of the nurses' station.

'Good grief,' Nola said when she saw it. 'Who's that for?'

'Pippa,' Jenny said. She peered at the little white card and took it off the plastic stick.

'Jenny!' Nola warned.

'It's stuck down with a heart.' Jenny said, and sighed. She went to put it back, though not quite in time, because Pippa emerged from the office. 'This came for you,' Jenny said.

'Do tell me who it's from,' Pippa said rather pointedly as she took the card from Jenny. But instead of opening it, she pocketed it in her scrubs.

'Who sent it?' Jenny asked.

'I'll find out when I get home,' Pippa retorted,

and then looked at the large plant, now taking up a lot of the desk. 'When the two of us get home. Heavens, look at the size of it!'

She stashed it in the office temporarily, and then headed into the drug room.

Luke worried that he was turning into Nosy Jenny, because he was dying to know what was in the envelope.

He was more than used to women and the games they played. A lover had once sent flowers to herself, pretending they were from an ex, in an attempt to make him jealous and nudge him to commit.

It hadn't worked.

This plant, though, must be a triffid. Because even though it had been put away, he could still see its shiny leaves, waving from the office door.

And, given how little time they had left, it niggled him that Pippa had been so vague about her plans tonight.

As her shift was about to end, he caved in and headed to the drug room.

'Your secret lover has terrible taste,' he said, when he found her.

Pippa laughed. 'My aunt sends me a plant every year. I don't know why she doesn't send it to my flat.' She glanced over. 'Don't tell Jenny who it's from.'

'Wait—it's your birthday?' he checked, and did a quick mental calculation, because if she'd been two years below him at school… 'Your thirtieth?'

'Don't remind me.'

'But why didn't you say anything?'

'I just didn't.' Pippa shrugged.

'So what are you up to?'

'I'm catching up with friends at the weekend.'

'But what about tonight?'

'Luke, I really don't make a fuss about birth-days.'

'Maybe *I* want to make a fuss.' He came a little closer than he usually would at work and named the very nice French restaurant just a short walk from his flat.

'I really don't need—' Pippa started, but then she took out her phone and saw that there was *still* no message from her parents. Hell, she wanted to celebrate her birthday—and for once there was actually someone who wanted to celebrate it too. 'I'd like that,' Pippa said.

'What about your plans?' Luke checked.

'They've changed.' Pippa smiled.

'Brilliant. Should I book it for seven?' he asked. 'I should be finished here in an hour or so.' He checked his pager. 'Maybe two. It might be better to meet there...'

'Sounds great.'

It really did.

It was the first birthday she'd dared even hope to celebrate like this, and she was rushing as she pulled off her scrubs and changed into jeans, her head full of what on earth to wear, wondering if she had time to hit the shops...

'Drama, drama!' Jenny said as she came into the changing room. 'Shona just called and asked to speak to Luke.'

'Who?'

'That ICU nurse from St Bede's.'

'You've lost me.'

'Shona—the one he had the affair with.'

'That's just gossip.'

'Oh, no, it's not,' Jenny said, pulling on the vast jumper she'd knitted. 'Fiona told me all about it. She caught them in the break room herself. Shona must have heard he's back in London. You should have seen Luke's face when I told him who was on the phone, asking to speak with him privately.'

Privately?

Pippa felt her heart sink—but then reminded herself how much she loathed gossip. And anyway, Luke had said himself that the rumours were false.

'He asked to take the call in Nola's office,' Jenny elaborated. 'His face was like thunder.'

Sure enough, she could see Luke on the phone in the office. The blinds weren't closed and, even though she tried not to look, Pippa could see the tension in his shoulders as he stood with his back to the ward, his hand raking through his dark hair.

'Told you!' Jenny said, clearly delighted with her gossip. 'Go in and get your plant. You might hear—'

'I've got to dash,' Pippa interrupted, unsure whether she was refusing to engage in gossip, or burying her head in the sand, or just selfish, because she wanted one perfect birthday with this man she had liked for far too long…

She decided she would leave the enormous plant at work overnight, so she could make it to the shops. In the end, she found a lovely lilac dress that was so soft she thought it was wool—but she looked at the label and saw it was silk.

And then she saw the price. Even though it was in the sale, it was still out of her league.

But then she was already playing way out of her league…

Yes, there was a fair chance Luke had looked her in the eye and lied about his past, but Pippa knew she too had been lying all along…pretending she belonged in a world of casual lovers and passion that came with no strings attached.

'Try it on,' the assistant suggested.

Perhaps she should have walked away in The Avery, or should walk away even now, yet she found herself in a cubicle, stripping down to her underwear and pulling the dress on over her head.

It was—unfortunately for her credit card—perfect.

She angled her head in the mirror, hoping she'd look dreadful from behind. But no, it was as if a thousand magical mice had been working on the gown all night.

It wasn't really a gown, but it made her think of Julia, in her silver ballgown, heading out for one fabulous night…

Well, Pippa would have one fabulous birthday!

Back in her flat, Pippa decided she would go all-out tonight and make a real effort.

She put loads of product in her hair, then hung her head upside down and tackled the diffuser. It took for ever, and even then her thick dark hair wasn't completely dry, but she was running out of time.

Pippa put on some make-up, as well as the fabulous underwear that she'd added to her purchase—and even stockings, heels and dangly earrings…

When she checked her reflection she worried that it was too much, and didn't suit her.

Because this night mattered more than any other ever had…

'Madame…' the greeter said, and smiled when she gave her name and then said something in French.

It took a second's delay to work out that he'd asked for her coat. Pippa handed it over and then was shown to a reserved table. A little unsure, she ordered a glass of red wine, but he stared at her blankly, so Pippa dragged out her schoolgirl French.

Her wine came with a little silver dish of nibbles.

The garlicky, herby scent was making her stomach rumble. She looked at the other couples there, and the pair of elderly ladies who were laughing as they went out for a cigarette.

The waiter was back, brandishing the wine bottle.

'No, I'm fine,' Pippa said. *'Non, merci,'* she corrected herself.

And only then did it enter her head that Luke might not be coming.

He wouldn't stand her up on her birthday, would he?

Unless something had come up at the hospital…?

But then surely he could have fired off a quick text?

No, he was a trauma surgeon, Pippa reminded herself. He was hardly going to ask one of the staff to message her; she was the one who had insisted on discretion after all…

There were so many arguments taking place in her head. She wanted to trust him, to believe it was nothing more than work delaying him. But the voice she had been trying to ignore chimed up a little more loudly.

Had the call from his ex derailed his plans for the night?

Finally, there came a text, and it felt as if every pair of eyes in the restaurant were on her as she read it.

Sorry. Talk later.

An apology, but no explanation.

Still, it told Pippa enough, and she signalled for the waiter.

'Could I have the bill, please?' He gave her a non-plussed look. 'You know exactly what I mean,' Pippa snapped, and to the waiter's credit he gave her a little smile, then headed off to fetch a velvet folder.

Pippa paid for the *extremely* expensive glass of red wine, and even added a tip because—well, she was burning with embarrassment.

No, it wasn't embarrassment. It was the disappearance of hope that *one* birthday, just one...

It was a long taxi ride home, with a thankfully quiet driver.

Behind closed doors, she peeled off her shoes and stockings and washed off all her make-up, then donned an over-sized T-shirt. She poured herself a far cheaper glass of wine than she'd had in the restaurant and moved her heated blanket from the bedroom to the sofa and curled up under it.

This was supposed to be fun —and yet it was starting to hurt.

It was close to ten when there was a knock at the door and Pippa knew it was Luke. She was tempted not to open it, but she knew that would be petty.

'Hey,' she said, trying to pretend it didn't really matter.

'I'm so sorry, Pippa, for leaving you stranded on your birthday.'

'Hardly stranded,' Pippa said as she let him in. 'I've been stood up in worse places.'

But then she saw his tense expression and watched as he sat on the couch, picked up her glass and took a drink.

'I got a call from St Bede's.'

'Shona?' Pippa nodded, refusing to skirt the issue. 'Jenny told me.'

'She's working on the ICU now.' He frowned, but then dismissed whatever thought he'd just had. 'Hamish collapsed.'

'Hamish?' Pippa felt a jolt of panic dart through her, but she remained perfectly still. 'You mean Darcy's twin?'

Luke nodded. 'Evan was already on his way to visit, and I had to go and tell Amber that he'd taken a sudden turn for the worse.'

'Oh, my God.'

'Amber was frantic. She didn't know what was happening. And, what with them being identical twins, she wanted me to check on Darcy—bloods, infection...'

Pippa nodded. It had been days since the accident, though, and hopefully the boys hadn't been brewing any infection or unknowingly sharing an undiagnosed condition. Of course it was vital to check, and only right that the doctors would be concerned for the healthier twin.

'Did you find anything?'

'No. Nothing related. It would seem that Hamish's brain bleed had extended.'

Pippa swallowed.

'I heard an hour or so ago that he'd died.'

She watched Luke put his head in his hands and felt goosebumps prickle her arms and even her bare legs as she stood there in nothing but her T-shirt.

She was helpless, waiting for Luke to correct himself, to say it had been a mistake, for the world to go back to a more correct order.

Luke must have noted her complete lack of response because he lifted his head. 'Are you okay?'

'I don't know,' Pippa admitted, a little stunned to see his face streaked with tears.

She took a seat on the couch beside him. She felt shaken up inside, but kept her breathing steady. 'Who's with Darcy?'

'An uncle or a cousin arrived to sit with him just as I left, although Darcy was asleep.'

'He knew,' Pippa said through pale lips. 'Darcy knew something was wrong…'

'Pippa—'

'He did.' Pippa was insistent. 'When Julia took a turn for the worse I felt ill all day at school.' She let out a sliver of her hurt. 'No one thought to call me to come home and say goodbye. I found out when I got back from school.' She looked over. 'It needs to be his parents who tell him—not his uncle.' Pippa's voice was urgent. 'My aunt was the one who told me and—'

'Pippa,' he interrupted. 'I'm sure Amber and Evan will tell him together; they just don't want him to be on his own tonight…' He frowned at her pallid face. 'I'm sorry to bring bad news.'

He took her hand, and although she wanted to cling to it, Pippa was scared by her own devastation and the dreadful memories it was unleashing.

She wasn't used to sharing her grief, and surely Luke, who was already clearly upset, didn't need his short-term lover to crumple emotionally.

'How was Amber?' Pippa asked.

'I told her well away from Darcy; Nola brought her into the office. I've had to give bad news to a lot of parents, but this one's really got to me.' He took a shaky breath and wiped his cheeks. 'Looks as if I'm like my father after all…'

'Meaning?'

'He's come home upset a couple of times. You'd never have guessed if you only knew him at work. I came downstairs once and found him crying. It scared the life out of me.'

'What did you do?'

'Offered to get my mother…' He looked over. 'She paints too…'

It was an odd moment for Luke.

To be sitting with the woman he realised he needed tonight.

And, while Pippa wasn't exactly effusive, she wasn't shut away in her studio like his mother. Instead, she sat beside him, pulling her T-shirt down over her knees…

It wasn't the wildest birthday for her.

Pippa lay on the sofa with her head in his lap, while Luke finished the wine.

Both were locked in their own thoughts.

But they were together.

And tonight, that meant the world.

* * *

Pippa would have hated to hear this news tomorrow, in hand-over. The dread that gripped her was similar to the way she'd felt when she'd been told Julia had died. She'd panicked when Luke had told her about Hamish, yet he didn't seem to mind.

She felt his hand still in her hair, and then heard his voice, which rarely revealed any uncertainty.

'I should have transferred Hamish. At least Darcy would have been with his brother.'

Pippa thought for a moment. 'And witnessed his collapse? Heard the resuscitation attempts? Seen him die?'

She shook her head, and then turned in his lap so she could see him.

'It would have been dreadful for Darcy. Aside from that, St Bede's is one of the best neuro hospitals. You did the right thing, keeping Hamish there. What if he'd died in the back of an ambulance?' She watched as he closed his eyes and finally accepted her words. 'By not bending to everyone's wishes and moving him, you gave him the best chance.'

'Thank you,' he said, 'for saying that.'

'It's the truth,' Pippa said with conviction. She moved up on his lap. 'You did the best you could—life just doesn't always play fair.'

'No,' he agreed. 'It doesn't.'

Luke looked at this woman whom he'd stood up tonight—there'd not been a single text demanding where he was…not one angry call.

'I'm sorry I ruined your birthday.'

'You didn't.' Pippa shrugged. 'I hate birthdays anyway.'

'Hate them?'

Pippa blinked, about to retract or cover up her statement. But yes, on this, her thirtieth birthday, thinking of little Darcy and poor Hamish, it felt safe to say she officially hated them.

'Yes.'

'Why?' Luke pushed. 'Do you mean since you lost—?'

'No.' She shook her head, because it wasn't all about Julia's death, and he'd been honest about how he was feeling, so she felt a little braver. 'I always hated them,' she admitted. 'I used to turn down friends' party invites.'

'How come?' he asked, his hands on her bare thighs.

He looked into green eyes that were finally a little less guarded than they'd been since the day they'd met.

'Julia couldn't go to parties, you see. Mum didn't think it was fair.'

'What about *your* birthdays?'

'Some were nice…' she said. 'My parents forgot my seventh birthday, though.'

'Totally forgot?'

'With good reason.' She told him how sick Julia had been, and about the nurse who had remembered at the eleventh hour. 'Maybe Julia told her,' Pippa mused. 'I don't know where she got that cake.'

Luke mulled this over. For all his father's faults, he'd never missed a birthday. Hell, even though they were still barely talking, he'd called the other night to check on him.

'So they don't bother with your birthday at all now?'

'There'll be a card with some cash next time I go over.'

He thought of her checking her phone in the drug room. 'Do they call?'

'Birthdays upset them,' Pippa said, in her parents' defence. 'No one can know how they feel unless they've lost a child.'

Luke swallowed down a slightly caustic reply, because it would be aimed at Pippa's parents rather than at her. He thought of Amber, about how desperate she had been to get to Hamish, and yet she had never for one second forgotten the son she was leaving behind and had begged Luke to check on him...

'Anyway,' Pippa said, shrugging, 'I don't make a big deal of them.'

He kissed her then, and Pippa kissed him back, chasing away the horrors of the day.

As he undressed, he saw Pippa reach into his jacket for a condom. Knew they were both urgent for escape.

They made love on the sofa, but it was necessary sex, to drown out the noise in their heads. It was passionate, rather than intimate.

But it was in the small hours of the morning that they ran into danger...

CHAPTER NINE

PIPPA WOKE BEFORE DAWN, and although Luke lay still beside her, she could feel he was awake.

'Can't sleep?' she asked.

'No,' Luke said, and then, 'You thought I was with Shona?'

Pippa realised that it wasn't only the sad events of the night keeping him awake.

'Tonight?' Luke persisted. 'You thought I was with her.'

'I didn't know what to think,' Pippa admitted. 'I *don't* know what to think.'

She stared up at the ceiling, asking herself who she was to play judge and jury over his past. But there were things that mattered…that were important to discuss.

'She was *married*, Luke.'

'So was my father…'

Her head turned to face him 'What?'

'It wasn't *me* having the affair.' In the darkness, they rolled over and faced each other. 'It was my father and Shona.'

'So why did *you* leave St Bede's?' Pippa frowned. 'Why did you take the fall?'

'I just knew I didn't want to be there any more. I'd lost all respect for my father. And Shona's husband worked on one of the wards. Nice guy…' He thought for a moment. 'I'd already been looking at studying in America, and that gave me the push I needed.'

He didn't speak for a moment, yet Pippa could feel he was still thinking.

'Truth be told, I was never one hundred percent sure I wanted to work there... That bloody chemistry exam!'

'Fragmentation,' she said, and he laughed and gave her a playful punch.

His hand remained on her arm and she could see his dark eyes shining...knew they were locked with hers. She felt closer to him than she ever had to another. Whispered conversations in the night with Julia didn't count, because this was very different. This was two adults confiding and sharing, being vulnerable, touching and supporting, letting the other in...

'How did you find out? About the affair, I mean?' Pippa said. 'Gossip, or...?'

'No. It would seem they were actually very discreet. That's why people thought it was Shona and me.'

He smiled at her frown.

'It was pure chance,' he explained. 'Just a couple of things. My parents and I didn't live in each other's pockets. When I started my residency, he was setting up a surgical department in a new hospital in the Middle East.'

'Your mother went with him?'

'Yes. They only came back a couple of years before I left St Bede's.'

'Was it odd?' Pippa asked. 'Working with him?'

'We didn't overlap much, though we were certainly operating within each other's orbit. Still, you know how tight-knit Theatre is?'

'I guess…' Pippa started.

But then she thought back to her training and nodded. Theatre, more than anywhere, had been its own separate world. She thought of her shoes squeaking on the sticky mats as she entered, the flap of doors behind her, and how the nursing staff, at least for the most part, even took all their breaks there.

'Yes,' she now agreed. 'Although since my training—apart from handing over a patient or picking them up in Recovery—I've never really been inside a theatre.'

'I'd heard him laughing a bit more vibrantly in Theatre—his "holiday laugh", I always call it, because he's a different guy when he's away from the hospital.'

'Nicer?'

'Mmm,' Luke affirmed. 'He lightens up a bit. But suddenly he started to seem a bit more cheerful at work.' He ran a hand down to her waist. 'Perhaps the same way *you've* been more cheerful at work of late.'

'No!' Pippa said, laughing. 'I'm hopefully more discreet than that.'

'You are. Though I guess they were discreet too…that was how they got away with it. If I hadn't been his son I'd never have known.'

'So how *did* you find out?' Pippa asked, and her interest was not so much in the affair but more in how Luke had worked it out.

Even if there was no future for them, she still wanted to know more about him—ached to know more and therefore get closer to this man who enthralled her.

He always would.

Even that inward admission startled Pippa a touch. All this time she'd been telling herself she could do this—could keep things light and enjoy their time together. Yet here they were, on a night like no other, wrapped in each other's bodies, and she was asking him to confide in her.

'You don't have to tell me...'

'That's just it,' Luke said. 'I've never told anyone. But I want to tell you.'

It was the same way he'd felt the need to come here tonight—not just to apologise for messing up her birthday, but because he'd needed to see her. And that was a very unfamiliar feeling, but one he'd chosen *not* to push aside tonight.

'I always get my parents theatre tickets for Christmas—well, I used to,' Luke explained. 'That year I'd got them tickets for *Hamilton*. Anyway, one morning I heard him humming a song from it in the changing room. I didn't have time to give it much thought. I had a big case that I was rushing to get to.'

'How long after Christmas were the tickets for?'

'March,' he said. 'I'd pretty much forgotten about it till I heard him humming, and I made a sort of note in my head to ask him if he'd enjoyed it. But then I remembered that my mother had been away with friends that weekend. I guess I figured they must have changed the tickets. To be honest, I didn't dwell on it. Shona was scrubbing in for me that morning, and I just asked her how come I hadn't seen her recently. Had she been avoiding me? That kind of thing. It was just a joke, but she went so red...'

Pippa was listening intently, and he was enjoying the closeness they shared as he told her his story.

'Then, a little while into the operation, someone asked her if she'd enjoyed *Hamilton* on Saturday. It all just clicked—his singing, him being in a good mood around Theatre more.'

'What did Shona say?'

'Nothing. She was passing me forceps and her hand froze. I looked up from the patient and saw she'd turned scarlet again.'

'You were certain just from that?'

'Shona couldn't even look at me. I realised that she really had been avoiding me—a guilty conscience, I guess. And I found out I was a really good surgeon that morning, because I just got on with the operation.'

'What about Shona?'

'She said she felt unwell and scrubbed out.'

'What a mess...'

He nodded. 'Once the patient was in Recovery, I went to the break room. She followed me in and started crying, grabbing at me and pleading with me not to say anything. Her husband's a senior nurse on the orthopaedic ward. A great guy. She was saying it would break his heart, and I was telling her she should have thought of that before...' He gave her a mirthless smile. 'You know my junior?'

'Fiona?'

'She was a med student then. She, along with a couple of others, walked in on us arguing. I just left. But, given that Shona was standing there crying, they thought I was breaking up with her, or whatever—that it was the two of *us* having an affair. It was a natural assumption, I guess, given that we're closer in age. My father's in his mid-fifties.'

'Gosh. Why didn't you...?'

Pippa's voice faded. The answer was obvious, perhaps, but to her it seemed so unjust that he'd taken the hit.

'I spoke to my father and told him exactly what I thought of him. My leaving wasn't about taking the blame for him, or anything like that. I just couldn't stand to be working alongside him, and nor did I want to work with Shona and face her husband every day, knowing what I knew, but not being able to say anything.'

'Is it still going on?'

'No idea. I haven't spoken to her since, apart

from professionally, and nor do I want to. That call earlier was about work. She's on the ICU now.'

'Did you tell your mother?'

'No. I'd already tried that once.'

'It wasn't your father's first affair, then?'

'It wasn't.' He was silent for a long moment before answering. 'I stayed out of it this time.'

'I'm sorry I said anything.'

'It's fine.' He shrugged and sighed. 'The rumours are everywhere. I'm no saint, but I told you, Pippa, that I'd never get involved with someone who was already in a relationship.'

'I know you did.'

'Why do you think I never want to settle down? Or get overly involved with anyone? I trust people, but I don't trust couples. I don't want the hurt or the lies that come, or how people pretend things are fine when they're clearly not.' He looked at her. 'I swore off serious relationships and marriage before I'd even made it to medical school—'

He stopped abruptly, as if the memory was something he did not want to revisit.

'Is that why you want to get out of London?' she asked.

Luke was about to nod, but he knew it wasn't really an honest answer, and it seemed they were all about honesty tonight.

'It certainly factors into my decision not to go back to St Bede's,' he said, then hesitated.

His decision to leave London had been set in

stone when he'd returned from the States—sell and get out. Yet now, having told Pippa, he realised that saying everything out loud and having her react so calmly had honestly helped. And, despite the gossip at The Primary, he was enjoying his time there.

London no longer felt like the closed-in, locked-down world from which he'd been so pleased to escape.

Pippa broke his silence. 'You'll be in Scotland soon,' she said. 'Well away from it all…'

'Why don't you come?' He saw her eyes widen. 'I mean, for a visit.'

'Why?' Pippa smiled. 'Because you'll be sex-starved in your little stone cottage?' she teased. And they laughed as they moved in closer to each other. 'Or so you can stand me up in Scotland too?'

'You're not going to let me live that down, are you?' he said, pushing her hair from her face. 'How long did you wait at the restaurant?'

'Half an hour.' She smiled. 'Okay, forty-five minutes, maybe? It was excruciating.'

'Why?' He pulled her closer to him. 'I often eat there alone.'

'In a new dress and dangly earrings at a table set for two?'

'On occasion,' he teased, his hand coming down to her bare arm.

'Did you really buy a new dress?' he asked.

'I did,' Pippa said, because making fun of being stood up in a gorgeous restaurant felt a whole lot better than everything else that had happened. 'And underwear.'

'Damn,' he said, then moved his hand to her smooth naked hips. 'And body lotion…'

'That's not new,' she said. 'I even wore make-up…'

'I'll make it up to you. Your next day off—our next mutual day off—I'll book and we can go again.'

'No way! I am never going back there,' Pippa said, laughing. 'The shame!' She thought of the awful waiter and then she met his eyes. 'It honestly doesn't matter.'

'It honestly does.'

Sometimes his kiss felt like an escape, a fantasy come true, or even a delicious glimpse of paradise—as if their mouths mingling somehow took her to another place. Only, in this pre-dawn morning it didn't feel like that. It felt as if she was exactly there, and so too was Luke. Both together in a place they had somehow made—a place that actually existed.

His kiss was different. Not the rough kiss of earlier, nor the decadent, sexy ones they often shared. This kiss was slower, yet deeper.

She opened her eyes and found that she was staring into his, the contact so probing and direct that she closed her eyes. She felt as if he could see right inside her soul, and if that was true then he might see that there was a place in it reserved only for him.

Yet even as she broke eye contact, still there was nowhere to hide in this bed, where deeper intimacies were being shared.

His hand moved behind her head, with a slight pressure that felt exquisite, and Pippa put her hand on his chest, feeling the soft mat of hair. Then she explored the side of his torso, running her hand down to his waist and relishing her slow perusal of his body as their tongues mingled.

They were soon wrapped around each other, and when she rolled onto her back it was so mutual that Pippa wasn't sure if it was his command or her body's beckoning. His thighs nudged hers apart and she lifted her knees. In her cold bedroom, the warmth they made together felt essential.

Pippa heard her own soft moan as he squeezed inside her. Luke had propped himself up on his elbows, but she could still feel his delicious body pinning her to the bed. He moved, slowly at first, but so deeply that she felt a tightening low in her stomach. Her thighs parted further to allow for more intensity.

'Pip…'

For the first time she didn't object to the shortening of her name. There was no breath left to waste on such irrelevancies anyway.

His pace did not increase, and yet with each measured stroke Pippa felt as if she was falling apart. Even as she tightened beneath him and turned her head from his kiss he would not let her hide, and he moved her head to face him. Pippa put up her hand to bring his head down, but he removed it and pinned her arms behind her head, then looked at her as he moved deep inside.

'Pippa…'

He was up on his forearms, and she knew he was asking her to look at him. She knew that even if she kept her eyes closed she would still be letting him in to that place reserved solely for him.

She was coming undone, starting to cry, sobbing his name, and still he did not relent—he only thrust deeper. His breath was hot on her cheek as he finally increased his speed, suddenly moving too fast for her to think. She was always thinking—but for a second all thought stopped. Her hips rose in an urgent and involuntary motion as she climaxed and felt him still. Then came his breathless moan, and as she ached with the end of her orgasm he took her straight back there again, reviving her intimate pulses as he came deep inside.

She could feel the sheen of sweat on his arms as he collapsed onto her, and the coolness of her own tears on her cheeks. She was silently appalled at her capitulation…at the fact that she'd let go as much as she just had.

And now her mind was back, trying to count how many times they had made love in their short time together. She scanned her memory…

Then she heard the bleep of his phone, and as he rolled off her Pippa knew, with absolute certainty, that she'd just made love for the very first time.

* * *

As his phone alarm demanded they part, Luke hit snooze for the first time since they'd been together.

'Pippa...?' He too sounded as if he had found himself in an alien world.

'What?' Pippa asked, perhaps a little abruptly. But she was trying to catch her breath, and was terrified by what had just happened between them.

He was going to tell her that things had got too intense, she was certain. Had he read in her eyes or felt in her body the love she'd been trying to hide? After she'd sworn not to love him.

'Pippa,' he said again. 'We didn't use anything.'

Oh, was that all?

In the grand scheme of things, it didn't seem as earth-shattering as her most recent realisation, Pippa thought. He was probably panicking in case his bachelor life was over.

'It's fine.' She looked back at him. 'I'm on the Pill.'

'Even so...'

'Luke, you're on call.'

It wasn't like ward round mornings when he could risk being a bit late. The pagers would be handed over, and it wasn't fair to anyone if he wasn't there.

'You need to get ready.'

He nodded and, like the secret soldier she had begun to suspect he was, he rolled out of bed. Thoughtful as ever, he turned on her electric blanket before heading to the shower.

Pippa tried to correct her thoughts. It couldn't be love because that took two, she reasoned. Still, it had been intense, that sudden move from safe sex—both figuratively and emotionally—to soft, slow sex.

She lay there as he used her tiny shower, feeling the tension that had lived in her for ever starting to return.

She was falling deeper into this man, when she'd honestly hoped that this month together might break the spell of him. Always before the gloss had worn off…always she'd backed off because they'd got too close…

This time, though, *she* was the guilty party.

Oh, where is my casual lover mask? Pippa thought as he came out of the shower and started to dress.

'We need to talk, Pippa,' he said as he knotted his tie. 'Look, I'm sorry I didn't take better care this morning. It hasn't happened before—I always wear protection—but I'm happy to go and get checked if it makes you feel any better.'

'Checked?' Pippa frowned and, despite the blanket starting to warm up, she felt the same goosebumps she had last night.

She felt a sudden sense of panic, as she wondered if he was asking if she carried the CF gene, and what his reaction would be if she told him she did.

But that wasn't what Luke was asking.

'If you're worried I've got anything…' He was matter of fact. 'Though I'm sure there's no problem.'

No problem? It wasn't the unprotected sex that was the problem…

She could deny it no more.

Luke Harris was back in her life and again he was taking over her heart.

CHAPTER TEN

SOME DAYS, PAEDIATRIC nursing was the best job in the world.

Others…

Evan was dealing with the awful practicalities that death brought, while Amber was in with the child psychologist, working out the best way to tell Darcy about his twin.

Pippa was just clearing his IVAC when the question came.

'Where's Hamish?'

'Why don't I get Mummy…?' Pippa started, but was saved from having to avoid the issue by fetching his mother because Amber had walked in.

'Darcy was just asking where Hamish was,' Pippa explained.

'Were you, Darcy?' Amber said as she limped over on her booted leg, taking a seat in what must be an extremely painful position on the edge of her son's bed.

'Would you like me to leave you?' Pippa offered, but Amber shook her head.

'Stay,' Amber said, and then took a deep breath and gently told her son the simple truth. 'Hamish has died, darling.'

'So when is he coming back?'

Pippa put her hand on Amber's shoulder to support the poor mother as she tried to do what was best for her remaining child.

She answered his question as simply as she could. 'He won't be coming back.'

'Ever?'

'Ever,' Amber said.

'Like when Yoyo died?'

'Yes,' Amber replied gently, stroking his hair and talking to Pippa. 'Yoyo was the boys' budgie.'

'Will Hamish go in a box in the garden too?'

'No. There's a special garden for people.' Amber's voice was shaking, and yet she was being so tender with her explanations. 'And when you're well enough, we'll go and visit the garden.'

'Is he there now?'

'No, not till next Friday,' Amber told him. 'Mummy and Daddy are going to go and say goodbye, and when you're well enough, and ready, we'll take you too.'

'You're crying, Mummy,' said Darcy, and his little hand went to her cheek.

'Because I'm sad. You'll be sad at times too, but that's okay. We'll look after each other and give each other cuddles... Can I have one now, please?'

As Darcy wrapped his arms around his mum's neck she hugged him back hard and then quietly addressed Pippa.

'Thanks,' she said. 'I think we'll be fine now.'

Very few things made Pippa cry. Actually, until Luke had brought her undone last night, nothing really had. But hearing Amber being so gentle with her son brought a rare flash of tears.

She sniffed them back and went to tell Nola,

along with Luke, who was updating his notes, that Darcy had now been told about his twin.

'Amber was really good with him,' Pippa said, and repeated what Darcy had said and his concept of death. 'He knows that his brother's...' She felt the unfamiliar sting of tears threaten again, and excused herself.

'You okay?' Luke checked, when he found her back in her default position of pouring boiling water on a teabag in the break room.

'I'm fine.'

'It's tough.'

'Yes,' Pippa agreed, unsure why she had used that tone of voice when he was just being nice. 'I'm going to have tea.' She added sugar and pulled out the teabag, and then added too much milk.

'Pippa,' he said, halting her, 'it's fine to be upset.'

'I know.' She nodded but then, desperate to escape his scrutiny, she walked off.

'Pippa!' he called her back. 'Can we talk about last night?'

She felt her back stiffen. It was as if last night she'd revealed a glimpse of her soul, and now she truly wished he hadn't.

'If there are any repercussions...' Luke said. 'I know you said you're on the—'

'Luke!' Her eyes flashed a warning. 'We're at work.'

'No one can hear us.'

To make extra sure, he closed the door.

'Someone might come in!'

'What? And catch us *talking*?'

He walked over to the large kitchen table and took a biscuit from a packet before leaning on it.

'Let's give them something to talk about. *Ooh, Luke Harris was eating a biscuit,*' he mimicked, *'and Pippa Westford was drinking tea.*'

She let out a soft laugh and knew she was being paranoid. And it wasn't her colleagues she was worried about catching them.

She was worried that Luke might see into her heart.

'You were upset when I mentioned getting checked. Did you think I meant for CF?'

He was trying to have a very sensible conversation, she knew. And because he was a doctor, and knew about Julia, he was facing it head-on.

'Is it a concern?' he asked, and she knew he was asking if she was a carrier of the gene.

'Luke, I've told you—there's nothing to worry about. My sister died of a congenital illness. And as if I'd leave contraception up to a guy...' She watched his eyebrow rise as she hit a little below the belt.

'Have you been tested?' he asked.

'I'm not going to have this conversation—and certainly not at work. Why would I open up with someone who won't even be here this time next week?'

'Pippa, I always said I was leaving.'

'You always did,' she agreed.

'It's actually next Saturday that my contract ends. I'm not flying off on the first plane out, but even so, it's best we address this now.'

She simply did not know how to be close to someone—to a man—and certainly not to one who was leaving. They were only ever supposed to be temporary. She took her Pill religiously, because she carried the gene, and the only person whose business that was, was hers.

'There's nothing to address,' she told him.

'Good,' he said, and turned to go.

But as he reached to open the door Luke apparently changed his mind.

'For the record, you haven't opened up at all…'

'Why would I?' she asked. 'You probably wouldn't remember if I did anyway.'

'Am I sensing some resentment here? Because I don't remember a conversation fourteen years ago?'

'Of course not!' she attempted, but she knew she'd raised the subject once too often, and this time Luke didn't let it go.

'Am I being chastised because I didn't fancy you when you were sixteen? That's not very MeToo of you…'

'Stop it!' She actually laughed. How was he able to do that? To make her laugh on what was a very sad day? In a way that made a harsh world a little softer somehow?

For both of them.

* * *

Luke knew she'd been in with Darcy, and that this morning would have been very hard, so he reeled in his own frustrations.

'I'm sorry I don't remember,' he said.

'It's fine. You told me you wanted to be a drummer…'

'I think you're mixing me up with someone else,' he said with a frown. 'I've never even played the drums.'

'It was definitely you. You'd been crying that day. Your eyes were all red.'

'Probably because I'd been swimming.'

'No.' She shook her head. 'You had double sport later that afternoon.'

'What? Do you have a super-memory, or something?'

Only where he was concerned, she thought ruefully.

But rather than admit to that, she shrugged.

'I don't know. Maybe I am mixing you up.'

She forced out a smile and remembered that they'd agreed upon fun times only. She'd told him and herself that she could do this…

She just wished she could convince her heart, but it was still busy furiously objecting.

CHAPTER ELEVEN

THEY TRIED TO get back to being casual lovers, but the genie refused to return to its bottle.

'Here,' Pippa said, as she entered his flat the next night, holding the massive pot plant. 'I've brought you a present.'

'Please, no...'

'Well, it was you who suggested I come straight here after my late shift,' Pippa reminded him. 'Anyway, it would take up half my flat. She does this every year.'

'Your aunt?'

'Yes, and every year I have to rehome a plant.' She deposited it in an alcove by the fireplace in the lounge. 'It looks nice.'

'I'll kill it,' he warned.

When he looked at the vast pot plant his smile faded as he realised why her aunt did this each year—no doubt to prompt her colleagues, or to push the reticent Pippa into revealing that it was her birthday.

It made his heart constrict, and he looked from the plant to her, but Pippa was all smiles.

'You said we had to walk the puppy.'

'So I did.'

It was frosty outside and Pippa said that she thought they might get snow.

'It's too soon for snow,' he said, as the little dog shivered, and pawed at Luke's legs every time he tried to put him down on the pavement.

He sighed as he gave in and picked the puppy up, and they walked around the corner to a small park, where they sat on a bench, hoping Sausage would wee on the grass. But still he scampered to be picked up.

'How was Darcy?' Luke asked.

While usually he tried to leave work at work, he couldn't help but enquire about this patient.

'He's drinking a little bit.'

'Still not eating?'

'No.'

'Is he talking?'

'Not really,' Pippa said. 'I think—' She halted.

'Go on.'

'He's just hurting.'

'Have you spoken to him?'

'Of course.'

'I mean, about losing your sister?'

'I'm hardly going to unburden myself to a five-year—'

'Pippa,' he warned, halting her prickly reply. 'We both know you're not going to *unburden* yourself to Darcy. Have you spoken to him?'

'No.'

He left it there, and watched as Pippa stared into the night.

'Are we okay?' he checked.

'Of course.'

'Did I scare you by asking you to come to Scotland?'

* * *

Gosh, Pippa thought, she really must be playing it cool if he thought *that* was what was on her mind.

'Nothing like that,' she said. 'It's a nice offer. I just…'

She flailed about for a reason to explain why she was stalling. How to explain without fully revealing that saying goodbye next week was going to be hard enough.

'The off-duty roster isn't up yet.'

'Fair enough.' He nodded at her casual reply. 'Good boy!' Luke cheered as the puppy finally did a wee, and then added for Pippa's ears only, 'Mind you, he squats like a girl.'

'I don't think they lift their legs until they're older.'

'The things you learn…'

And they were back… Back to protected sex and laughter…back to cramming everything in.

Jenny had had some spare tickets to an interactive theatre production which Pippa had bought from her.

'I have no idea what it's about,' Pippa told Luke as they were admitted.

'I'd better not get tickets to this for my parents,' Luke said jokingly as they walked from room to room, watching the most torrid scenes.

There was an awful lot of nudity—full-frontal and everything.

'Good heavens!' Luke exclaimed as they stepped

back into the night. 'Are you trying to corrupt me, Pippa Westford?'

'Blame Jenny,' Pippa said.

They stood facing each other and she put her arms up on his shoulders.

'It was fun,' he admitted. 'Though I'm not quite sure what it was supposed to be.'

'Maybe you *should* get tickets for your parents…'

'Maybe…' He gave a half-smile. 'Did I tell you my father called me? That he wants us to go for a drink?'

'No.' Pippa shook her head. 'Will you go?'

'I don't know.' Luke shrugged.

Try as Pippa might, she still couldn't get the genie back in his bottle. And sometimes she forgot to keep things casual.

'I'd kill for my mum to call me and ask me to go for a drink,' Pippa admitted. 'Luke, he clearly cares about you.'

And sometimes Luke, too, forgot not to go in too deep. because as they stood outside the theatre, instead of kissing her, or hailing a taxi to take them back to his flat, he asked the question that had plagued him for years.

'Then why does he play Russian Roulette with his marriage?'

'It's *his* marriage he's dicing with,' Pippa said. 'You'll always be his son. Talk to him.'

'We'll see…' He looked right at her. 'Have you ever told your parents how you feel?'

'No,' Pippa admitted.

'Isn't that a little hypocritical?'

'True.'

She laughed, and so did Luke.

They were safely back on track…

Bound for nowhere.

CHAPTER TWELVE

KIM WAS GIVING the night hand-over.

'Luke suggested that the parents bring in his favourite takeaway for Darcy.'

Pippa raised her eyebrows, because she'd rather thought she'd gleaned his stance on that a few weeks ago. 'Did he eat it?'

'No.' Kim sighed. 'Well, one little French fry. But he wasn't really interested. The parents have to go and meet with the undertakers this morning. They want to do that together, but they're worried about leaving him.'

Nola looked over to Pippa. 'Can you special him today?' she asked. 'I'll give you Cot Four as well, but she's got her mother with her and is due to be discharged. I won't give you anyone else—well, not if I can help it...'

Darcy had refused breakfast and much to his mother's upset didn't seem remotely fazed when she kissed him goodbye before going to meet her husband.

'I can help Darcy with his lunch,' Pippa said to Amber as she filled a bowl from the sink to wash him. 'If you need a little longer.'

'Thank you,' Amber responded anxiously, and then gave Darcy another kiss before leaving.

Pippa followed her outside. 'I'll call you if he needs you, I promise, so take all the time you need.'

'What time are you on till?'

'Four,' Pippa said. 'I can push it till five, though, if necessary.'

'We have to take in an outfit…' Tears started streaming down Amber's face and Pippa guided her into one of the side rooms. 'I can't bear it, Pippa.'

Pippa put her arms around her as she wept for a moment.

'I don't want Darcy to see me like this.'

'I know,' Pippa said, admiring Amber for being able to cry gently with her son, but not so much that it scared him.

'I feel like I've lost Darcy too,' Amber sobbed. 'He barely speaks…'

'It's early days,' Pippa soothed.

But then she thought of what Luke had said and knew—or rather felt—that it was right for her to step up. As well as that, she had her second interview for the PAC Unit tomorrow, and wanted to test out if she could bring her very private past into work.

'I lost my sister,' Pippa told Amber, and she felt her go still in her arms. 'I was much older than Darcy, and we weren't twins, but there's such a bond…'

'Was it sudden?' Amber gulped—polite responses were forgotten when you were drowning in grief.

'No.' Pippa shook her head. 'But I remember being seven and nearly losing her.' She looked at Amber. 'Do you want me to try talking to Darcy? He might be scared of upsetting you.'

'Please,' she said, shivering. 'But only…'

'I'll be gentle,' Pippa reassured her. 'You go and see Hamish.'

Pippa was washing Darcy from top to toe.

'Your bruises are turning yellow,' Pippa said as she rinsed his little back. 'You look like you've been fighting with paint!'

She turned him onto his back and knew her light-hearted chatter wasn't helping. She tried to remember being five, but it was all a bit of a blur.

She'd loved nursery—that she did remember—and she recalled coming home and finding her mother crying in her bedroom…and her selfish wish that she'd still be able to go to the nativity play that night. That her mother would stop crying and that things would be okay…normal…

Whatever normal was.

It was lunchtime, and Darcy was gagging on a spoonful of mashed potato, when Pippa put down the spoon and spoke to him.

'I'm so sorry you're hurting, Darcy.'

He looked down at the dressings on his tummy.

'I meant here,' Pippa said, and tapped his little chest. 'Your heart's hurting. That's how I felt when my sister died.'

He didn't answer, but his big grey eyes didn't pool with tears, and for the first time they properly met hers.

'You're going to be okay, Darcy,' Pippa said, gently but firmly, in case he was scared that he might be about to suddenly die to.

Then she thought of what she'd used to wish for most in the world—Julia too.

'Mummy and Daddy are going to be okay, too. They're very sad, but they will be okay.'

She knew in her heart that in Darcy's case this was true. His parents were doing everything they could to take care of both their little boys.

'They love you so much.'

And then he said some words that cut through her heart. 'I want Hamish.'

'I know you do.' Pippa nodded. 'I wanted Julia— that was my sister—so badly after she died. She was the only person I could really talk to. She was my best friend.'

Darcy nodded, as if she'd finally said something he understood.

'I was so sad, and I needed her so much, but she wasn't there any more.'

He started to cry, and Pippa cuddled him and let him weep.

'You can always tell Mummy and Daddy when you feel sad.'

'But then *they'll* cry.'

'And that's okay,' Pippa said. 'Mummy has said to you that you can all be sad together, but I promise you will smile and laugh too, even if you can't believe that now.'

Darcy pulled back, and Pippa thought that she

herself was going to cry when he picked up his teddy bear. 'I want Hamish to have Whiskers.'

'What about Coco?' Pippa carefully asked, referring to his brother's bear.

'I want Hamish to have Whiskers *and* Coco.'

She held on to the teddy for a moment and looked at the bear's glassy eyes. She knew this was something for Amber and Evan to negotiate.

Then she looked at Darcy who, now he had cried, was ready to sleep. 'Why don't you cuddle Whiskers for now?'

'And then Hamish can have him?'

'No!' Amber was aghast at the idea.

She'd returned from the undertaker's holding Hamish's bear, Coco. Nola was there, and Luke, who was writing up some notes on another child, just happened to be in the office. He had put down his pen and was listening.

Amber was adamant. 'I've brought Hamish's bear for Darcy to have. They should be together.' Her eyes flashed at Pippa, loaded with accusation. 'What on earth did you say to him?'

Luke watched quietly, wincing inside when Amber reared, but Pippa took it well.

'I told him how I felt when I lost my sister.' Pippa had already reported back on the conversation she'd had with Darcy, and she responded calmly. 'Giving Hamish his own bear was Darcy's idea.'

Evan took his wife's hand. 'Darcy wanted him

to have it even before Hamish…' He couldn't complete the sentence.

'But he might regret it.' Amber looked to Nola, who gave a small nod, and then to Luke, who opened his mouth and then closed it again.

'What if he changes his mind?' Amber demanded. 'What do I tell him then?'

'He wants to do this for Hamish,' Pippa reiterated. 'He's going to be sad and upset, whatever you decide. He's always going to miss his brother.'

'I don't know what to do,' Amber sobbed into Hamish's bear.

'Pippa's right,' Evan said.

'There's no right or wrong in this situation,' Pippa said, and took a breath. 'But I think Darcy wants to do something for his brother. Why don't you go and see him with both bears, and talk to him about it?'

Nola stood. 'I'll take you to him.'

Nola helped Amber stand, and Pippa watched as Evan pulled some tissues from the box on the table and wiped his eyes before putting his arm around his wife as they headed off to see their son.

'Thank goodness you answered,' Luke said, taking up his pen. 'I had no idea what to say.'

'They're so good with him,' Pippa said. 'In all their grief for Hamish, they still think of Darcy every step of the way.'

'They do,' Luke agreed. 'What were your—?'

He halted, knowing this wasn't the time or

place—especially when the ever-indiscreet Jenny came in.

Then again, Luke thought, it was never the time or place when it came to Pippa…

'Nola's crying her eyes out in the loo,' Jenny informed them.

'Yes,' Luke responded gruffly, feeling a bit choked up himself. 'We've just had the Great Teddy Bear Debate, so go easy on Nola.'

'I know,' Jenny said, pulling some tissues from the same box that Evan had used and blowing her nose. 'She told me…'

To Luke's surprise, the formidable Jenny sat on one of the chairs and started to cry.

'I might crochet something,' Jenny suggested. 'For both of them.'

'That's a lovely idea,' Pippa said, and went and sat on the armrest. She shot Luke a quick *yikes* look. 'But I think that's something for the parents to work out.'

She gave Luke a small smile as she put an arm around Jenny, and it hit Luke then that he still didn't get Pippa. Okay, he didn't know Jenny's past, and he understood that Nola might be emotional…but, hell, even the hardened Luke felt moved by the parents' plight. Yet the one member of staff who should be dissolving, wasn't. The person who had lost a sibling, and who had dealt with Darcy's questions, as well as the distraught parents, was sitting on an armrest, comforting Jenny, when surely she must be in agony.

'Go home,' Jenny said to Pippa, while blowing her nose. 'You're supposed to be finished. You're off tomorrow, aren't you?'

'Yes,' Pippa said. 'Then back for nights.'

And Luke was stuck here.

'See you,' she said, and smiled at him just as she would if it were Martha, or Nola, or anyone else sitting in the office.

He nodded, and when Pippa had gone he flashed a smile to a still watery-eyed Jenny. 'I'll give you some privacy...'

Luke caught up with Pippa at the elevators. 'Are you okay?'

'Of course.'

'Amber didn't mean—'

'Luke, I do know what to expect from grieving parents.'

'Of course,' Luke said, but he knew how tough it must have been. Still, clearly Pippa didn't want to talk about. 'I've booked the restaurant for Saturday.'

'What restaurant?'

'The French one.'

'No way!' Pippa shot out a laugh.

'Well, I might have something to celebrate. Your pot plant seems to be working. I've got a couple coming back for a second look on Friday.'

'Fingers crossed,' Pippa said, wishing her lift would hurry up and arrive.

She was still in the land of teddies, and not up to

being flirty and fun—and as well as that she had art class tonight, and was really not in the mood.

'What are you up to tonight?' she asked him.

'I might go for that drink with my father,' he said. 'Can't keep putting it off.'

'Well, I hope it goes well,' Pippa said as her elevator arrived. It didn't feel quite enough. 'He is clearly trying…' she started, but then she reminded herself that what they had was fun, casual, flirty, and most of all temporary. Instead, she only said, 'Good luck.'

'Thanks,' he said. 'Enjoy your class!'

Tonight it was guided art, and they all attempted to follow the teacher and paint a view of Santorini… Only Greek islands and oil paint weren't the best mix for Pippa's dark mood.

The scent of paint and turps reminded her so much of art class back when she was at school, and how she'd mourned not just Julia but also Luke. And the thought of hurt soon to come turned the gorgeous Aegean Sea an ominous grey, and made the little fluffy white cloud over the domed buildings dark…

'Wow,' Cassie said as she came round to inspect her work. 'There's some storm brewing in Santorini!'

There was.

Taking her painting home, she was ridiculously desperate to stop at Luke's. She wanted to make a stupid joke as she handed over her painting…only she couldn't pretend for much longer that she wasn't falling apart on the inside.

She wanted to tell him her fears about the interview tomorrow. And to sob her heart out about Darcy…to be in Luke's arms when she told him how hard it had been to relive the confusion and terror she'd felt as a child.

But he was leaving soon…

And, no, she didn't want a couple of weeks in Skye to visit him and prolong the agony…

He might be trying to get closer to her, but Pippa was certain that if Luke knew the magnitude of her feelings he would break the sound barrier running away.

Pippa loved him.

She didn't feel sixteen all over again, when she'd felt so lost and alone.

Pippa felt thirty and adrift…

And dreadfully, scarily in love with Luke.

CHAPTER THIRTEEN

'PIPPA!' LUKE SMILED in recognition and then, looking at her unusually smooth hair, all neatly tied back, he frowned. 'You look very smart.'

'Thanks.'

'I'm guessing you're not up in Human Resources to sort out your leave or your pay?'

'Sorry…?' She frowned. and then gave a small shake of her head. 'Oh! No, I'm not.' She glanced up at the time. 'I really have to go…'

'Good luck,' he called.

Pippa swung around and frowned.

'For your interview.'

Pippa gave a wry smile. 'Has Nola been gossiping again?'

'I don't think so. At least, she didn't say anything to me.' He put his head on one side in a knowing gesture. 'Just a guess. I know interviews for the new wing are taking place at the moment.'

He looked down at the grey dress she had worn on their first date, now styled more formally with heels and such.

'I'm surprised you didn't say anything.'

'I haven't got the job yet. I messed up the first interview.'

His eyes widened. 'So this is your second?'

'Yes.'

'Yet you never mentioned it?'

Pippa knew it was quite an omission, and she could see he was a touch offended—possibly even hurt.

'We're not a couple,' she pointed out. 'You said at the start—'

'That was at the start, Pippa! Things have changed—or at least I thought they had. We were talking about Scotland…or I was… Hell, I've told you things I've never discussed with anyone—ever. And you've told me…' He looked upwards then, as if scanning back over all their conversations, their moments, their time. 'Nothing.'

'That's not true.'

'It's close,' he said. 'Because if I hadn't already known about Julia you'd never have said anything.' He took a breath. 'Look, I'm not going to get into this discussion now, because you've got an interview. Is it for Nola's job?'

'No.' She raked a hand through her hair. 'It's for the PAC Unit. Paediatric—'

'I know what PAC stands for.' He nodded, and then, because he did know about Julia, he seemed to understand immediately why she might want to work there. 'You can't have done that badly if they've called you back.'

'Believe me, I wasn't expecting them to. The first interview really was a bit of a disaster. I just…'

'What?'

'Clammed up,' Pippa admitted, 'and gave bland answers.'

'Of course you did.' He gave a wry smile.

'What does that mean?'

Her voice was defensive, she knew, but then her shoulders dropped. Because she also knew he was speaking the truth.

'I'm scared of saying the wrong thing,' she admitted, but it was only half an admission. 'I'm dreadful at conflict.'

'Good!' Luke said, and made her blink. 'Do you really think they want to hire someone who thinks they're brilliant at conflict? That's a red flag if ever there was one!'

She gave a reluctant smile. He made a very good point.

'And you are good,' he added. 'You stood up to Jenny when she was being mean about a mum...'

'That's not conflict.'

'It doesn't have to be a boxing gloves situation to be considered conflict.'

He'd made her feel better—at least, he'd stilled her racing heart enough for her to admit her greatest fear.

'I'm worried I might get overly emotional if I...'

'Pippa, I can't even imagine...' He paused, looking around him. 'How long till the interview?'

She glanced at her phone. 'Fifteen minutes.'

'You're early for once! You must really want this job?'

'Yes.'

'Try opening up a bit, Pippa.'

'I don't know how,' she admitted, but then she shook her head. 'I can't do this.'

'Yes,' he said, as if he'd decided that it had to be now. 'You can.'

He steered her out of the main traffic of the corridor and to the side of some vast noticeboard displaying plans for the new wing of the hospital.

And maybe it was because she really wanted the job, or perhaps because Luke Harris was so incredible that he could somehow manage to stop clocks as well as her heart, she decided that he was right, and maybe she could share a little of her fear.

It was more terrifying to be here than in the interview, standing in front of Luke, about to admit a deep and painful truth.

'Everything leads back to Julia…'

'Of course it does.'

She blinked at his matter-of-fact response, but then shook her head. 'I don't want to walk into an interview and get upset, or…'

'Show yourself?'

'I didn't say that.'

'No, *I* did. Pippa, it's not just in interviews. You hold back all the time.'

Luke was wondering if now really was the right time for this conversation. He knew she held herself back. In truth, her reluctance to get emotionally involved with anyone had appealed at first. After all, wasn't that perfect for a temporary relationship?

Only he felt that now he had become emotionally involved, perhaps more than he wanted to be—or more than Pippa wanted him to be. He'd seen her.

He'd seen the Pippa behind the barriers she put up—or perhaps it would be more accurate to say that he'd *glimpsed* her at times. Not just in bed, but sometimes when she looked up and smiled, or when they sat waiting for a puppy to wee… And the real Pippa, when she wasn't hiding, was so direct and so stunning that she really had blown him away.

'I know why they called you back,' he told her.

'Why?' Pippa frowned.

'Because they saw that there was more.' He thought for a moment. 'Of *course* everything goes back to Julia. How could it not? The things that happen to us—'

'Define us?' She almost sneered. 'Shape us?'

'No.' He shook his head. 'But we learn from them. Why do you think I've sworn off relationships and refuse to rely on anyone else?'

'That's not learning, Luke.' She gave an impatient shake of her head. 'Your parents' marriage makes you swear off relationships for life. That's hardly learning…'

'I'm just trying to say…'

He closed his eyes in frustration—not only because she was right, but also because she was wrong! Lately, thanks to Pippa, he *was* learning that things weren't all black and white.

'Okay, I'm not the best example, but you have learnt from your family—'

Pippa cut in with the truth then. 'I'm scared I'll break down.'

'Okay…'

'I haven't cried…not really. Not since…'

'Since…?'

'I honestly can't remember. Since I was four, maybe, or five,' she admitted. 'And I don't want it to be at work, and I certainly don't want it to be in there.'

She pointed to the interview room and Luke looked down the corridor. He'd known she was closed off, but hadn't realised just how serious it was.

She hadn't cried since she was four or five?

'You could postpone the interview,' he suggested. 'I'll even write you a doctor's note!'

'I don't want to postpone it.'

'Okay…' He had a think. 'You did well with Amber and Darcy.'

'Because I was worrying about them—not me.'

'Okay, worst-case scenario, maybe you'll cry a bit if you talk about Julia. Just don't boo-hoo.'

'That's far from my worst-case scenario!' she dismissed. 'Thanks for the sage advice, Luke.'

'Pip, listen to me.' He touched the top of her arm. 'You can talk about your sister if you're up to it, but the moment you've had enough, you stop it right there.'

'How?'

'Oh, what did you say to me?' He smiled. 'That night in The Avery? Something like, *"I don't want to talk about it."* It doesn't matter if it's an interview—you still get to say that.'

She chewed her lip doubtfully, but Luke had enough confidence for them both.

'Look how you've helped Darcy and his parents.' He gave her a soft smile. 'The teddy debate…'

She nodded.

'I had no idea what to say.' He was shepherding her towards the interview room now. 'I doubt many would.'

'There's no right or wrong…'

'Sometimes there is,' Luke said, thinking of his own ineptitude when it came to certain conversations. 'You're good at knowing it.'

It was Pippa who frowned now, but as they reached the bench where she was to wait, he snapped his fingers to get her attention back.

'You could help guide them because you've been there.'

'I haven't lost a child…'

'You were speaking up for Darcy,' he said. 'And you were good at that.'

'What if I—?'

'Worst-case scenario?' he checked.

'What if I lose it?'

'If you're really about to crack, then say one of your contact lenses has fallen out and excuse yourself,' Luke suggested. 'Though I doubt it'll come to that.'

She nodded.

'Okay. Just go in there and show them the real Pippa…'

'Philippa.' She gave him a wry smile. 'They keep calling me Philippa. It's very off-putting!'

'Then tell them you prefer Pippa.' He gave her a squeeze on the arm. 'Best wishes, Pip.'

'Not good luck?' she checked.

'It's not luck you need. Just be yourself.'

'What if they don't want that?'

'Then it's their tough luck.'

'Come through, Philippa.'

It was quite a panel that Pippa found herself facing, but before taking her seat in front of them she took a breath.

'Actually, most people call me Pippa.' She sat down. 'Except my parents when they're cross.'

She was prepared for all their questions, and she also went through her nursing experience and said how keen she was to be part of the start of a new venture.

'Yet I see that you only applied recently,' one of the directors interrupted. 'We've been advertising for some time.'

'I wanted to be very sure,' Pippa admitted. 'There was an Acting Unit Manager role on my ward. However, I realised I didn't want to apply for a caretaking role. If I'm going to be a unit manager, then I'd want to make the role my own.'

'It would be a demanding role,' the director said, and then quizzed her on what she'd achieved in her previous roles relating to standards.

Pippa had practised, so she answered more

smoothly this time. Then came the awful conflict question again.

'How do you deal with it?'

'I try to avoid it,' Pippa admitted wryly, and instead of it being the completely wrong answer she saw that a couple of them smiled. 'It's probably my weakness—personally, that is—but professionally, I know there are times when you can't avoid it.'

'What about angry parents?'

'Most of the time they're more upset than angry,' Pippa said. 'Or frustrated. Or scared...' She spoke from the heart, rather than from the cheat sheet she'd memorised. 'I think moving them away from the child—'

'That can be hard to do.'

'Not usually.' Pippa shook her head. 'I've generally found that if you tell the parent that a conversation might be better had away from their child, most agree, and then you can hopefully address whatever it is really concerning them.'

'Okay.' It was Miss Brett's turn now. 'What would you like to see implemented on the PAC Unit?' she asked, then took off her glasses and stared at Pippa. 'If you were given carte blanche, and could do anything at all?'

Pippa thought of Luke, urging her to be herself, and it made her feel brave enough to answer once again from her heart.

'I'd have a study area,' Pippa said, 'for siblings.' She saw Miss Brett blink. 'And a lounge, perhaps.

Somewhere they can charge their phones, take a break, be apart but not far away....'

'A study area for siblings?' Miss Brett frowned, but it wasn't a dismissive frown, more an interested one. 'Why do you suggest that?'

'I had a very ill sister,' Pippa said. 'She died when I was sixteen.'

'I'm so sorry,' Miss Brett offered, and there was moment of silence, but not a strained one, as Pippa nodded to her offer of water.

'Thank you,' Pippa said.

'Do you mind us asking how old your sister was when she died?'

'Eighteen,' Pippa said. Her voice wavered, but she chose to push on, ready to talk a little about Julia. 'She'd just been accepted into St Andrew's to study History.'

Pippa gave a fond smile, but as she thought back to that time she found it was a double-edged sword. The fond memories of her sister were tinged with her own private heartache that she'd hidden so fiercely until now. She thought again of what Luke had said, about showing her true self, speaking up...

She felt a pinch in her nose that signalled tears. 'Excuse me,' she said, and took out a tissue and blew her nose, then forced herself to speak on. 'I didn't do very well at school—at least not as well as I'd hoped to.' She wanted to explain better...to speak honestly about that time. 'I was always behind with homework and catching up. My sister's illness took precedence—of course it did.'

'How were your parents?'

'Julia was their world,' Pippa said. 'She still is...'

Miss Brett gave her a long, assessing stare. 'They haven't got over it?'

'No. There was bereavement counselling offered, but they never...' She couldn't quite go there, and neither did she want to. 'I really don't want to go into that here,' Pippa said.

Luke was right—she didn't have to.

She turned the conversation back to the interview, though with a personal slant. 'I don't know if there's anything the hospital staff could have done to change the trajectory for my parents, but I do know how the kindness and thoughtfulness shown to me by them meant the world.'

'It's very easy for the well sibling, or siblings, to get lost,' Miss Brett said, nodding. 'Overlooked...' She paused and thought for a long moment. 'A study area for siblings...' She turned to another member of the panel and asked to see the floor plans for the unit, then looked back to Pippa. 'Their own locker, perhaps? Or at least some stationery supplies.'

'And a printer,' Pippa said, and felt her heart start to hammer as she realised her suggestion was being taken seriously.

Then they moved on to speak about their prospective patients, the variety in their ages and conditions. How teenage boys with fragile bones who shouldn't be getting into fights all too often did. How an appendix didn't care if you were already a cancer patient—it just flared up.

It didn't feel like an interview any more, more like an exchange of ideas, and when it concluded Pippa felt that even if she didn't get the position there might still be a study room for siblings incorporated into their plans.

And birthdays would hopefully be remembered.

'How did it go?'

Luke was waiting for her outside.

'It went well, I think.'

'Did you tell them about…?'

'Luke!' She put her hand up to stop him, still attempting to hold herself together.

And then she remembered something she hadn't asked him earlier because she had been so focused on the interview.

'How did things go with your father last night?'

'They didn't.'

'You cancelled?'

'I never asked.'

'But—'

It was Luke's turn to raise a hand, warning her to leave it.

'We should apply for jobs as traffic controllers,' Luke said, and made her laugh. 'Let's go to The Avery.'

They went to the bar this time, rather than the restaurant.

'What do you want?' he asked.

'Champagne,' Pippa said.

'Celebrating?'

'No, I'm just spending your money while you're still here,' she teased.

'Pardon?'

'It was a joke!'

'I didn't hear what you said.'

She went on tiptoe and got an extra dose of his citrussy scent. 'I said…' She cupped her hand and whispered into his ear, 'I'm just spending your money—'

'Enjoy!' Luke said, laughing. 'That dress is making me think unholy thoughts,' he told her, and looking down she saw it was starting to gape. He picked up a strand of previously straightened hair, which was now starting to curl. 'We could take a bottle to yours…'

'I like it here,' Pippa said.

Nice loud music…where you almost had to shout to be heard. So loud that if she blurted out that she loved him, or begged him not to go, he'd put his hand to his ear and ask, *What did you say?*

Safe.

CHAPTER FOURTEEN

'No way that's Santorini.'

Luke was ready for work and pulling on his jacket while looking at her attempt from art class the other night.

'It's like a Goya painting,' Luke went on, referring to an artist known for his rather morbid paintings. 'Thank goodness I didn't give you free range on decorating the apartment.'

'I like it,' Pippa admitted.

'I'll see you tonight at work?'

'Yep.'

Luke peered out through her flimsy curtains at the grey sleet and shivered at the dismal sight. 'What a horrible day for a funeral.'

Was there ever a good day to have one? Pippa thought, but didn't say.

When he'd gone, she turned her blanket up to high, set the timer for six hours and deliberately went back to sleep.

It was exhausting being an upbeat, casual lover.

There was pall hanging over the ward when she arrived for her night shift.

The children and babies were oblivious, but Hamish's funeral had been held today and there was an air of sadness amongst the day staff. Pippa could feel it when she stepped into the office for hand-over.

Pippa was in charge of the night shift, and after taking hand-over, even though Darcy wasn't her patient tonight, she popped her head in and saw that he was asleep. In place of Whiskers there was a tatty purple dinosaur. Amber was sitting in the recliner, staring at nothing.

'Hi, Amber.' Pippa went over and sat on a stool by the chair. 'Is there anything I can get for you?'

She shook her head.

'I've made up a bed for you in one of the offices,' Pippa told her. 'If you need a break…'

'I want to be here whenever he wakes up.'

'I know you do, but if you or your husband want to take a short break then at least you'll have somewhere private. Do you want me to show you where it is?'

Amber nodded and hauled herself up from the recliner, and they walked in silence past the nurses' station and down the side corridor.

'It's tucked away,' Pippa said, opening up the door.

'I might lie down for half an hour,' Amber said. 'I've got the worst headache…'

'Of course.'

'Evan's coming in a bit later. He's with family at the moment.'

She was in a daze, and looked so utterly drained that when she sat on the low bed Pippa lifted her legs for her and helped Amber to lie down.

'Hamish has Whiskers and Coco. I think it was the right thing to do.'

'I do too,' Pippa said, and sat on the little bed. 'You listened to Darcy, and that's the most important thing for any child.'

'I'm sorry about your sister.' Amber looked at her. 'I didn't it say before.'

'I know you are.' Pippa gave her hand a little squeeze. 'I'll come and get you if Darcy wakes up.'

She flicked off the light and the door had barely closed before she heard deep sobs coming from the grieving mother—the saddest sound in the world, and one Amber had fought to protect Darcy from.

Pippa wanted to cry too.

She wanted to curl up and cry—for Hamish and his family, for her sister, and also because Luke would very soon be gone. Tonight was his final shift, and Pippa knew that soon she'd have to reset her heart and start all over again.

'Hey…' He came down to the ward about eleven. 'How are they all?'

'Amber's asleep in one of the back offices,' Pippa said. 'I think Evan will be in soon.'

'How's Darcy?'

'Worn out,' Pippa said. 'He had some supper, though.'

Luke checked the labs on a couple of patients, then stopped back at the nurses' station and leant on the desk overlooking her.

'Do you want a puppy?'

'My mother warned me about men like you.' Pippa laughed. 'Seriously…?'

'My neighbour has decided that Sausage is too

much responsibility. She's taking him back to the breeder.' He gave her a smile. 'Maybe we're kindred spirits.'

'Maybe.' Pippa smiled back, but it faded when it dawned on her that he was suggesting that he and his irresponsible neighbour were the kindred spirts, not him and her.

'Come over in the morning?' he proposed, but Pippa shook her head.

'I'll be tired.'

'Later, then? I still owe you a dinner...'

'French champagne to toast your last shift here?' she said, and hoped he missed the slight twist to her words.

'I think I can manage that. Then we can go back to mine for a proper celebration—and no having to get up at the crack of dawn to make the bed!'

'You've sold the flat?'

'Tentative offer.' He smiled, but she didn't quite know how to return it.

All his loose ends were being tied up and he would soon be gone. How could she toast that with champagne? Could she really keep up the pretence of not being emotionally involved until he left?

She needed to stay strong.

'I don't know if I can. I promised my parents I'd go over—'

'Pip,' he interrupted, and at the pursing of her lips checked himself. 'Pippa. If I remember rightly— and I do—you were lying to avoid your parents on the day we first met. Don't do the same to me. What's going on?'

Pippa closed her eyes and took a breath, then opened them. 'Okay, then. I don't like goodbyes.' It was only the tiniest fraction of what she was feeling. 'I don't know if I can sit there, raising a glass…' She tried to keep to the deal they had made. 'We've had a great month…'

Luke saw that she didn't meet his eyes.

He came around the desk and took a seat next to her. 'I'm not on the next plane out of here. In fact, I asked you to take some time off and join me.'

'I know you did.'

'And you still haven't answered.'

'What's the point, Luke?'

'Time away from here?' he suggested. 'A holiday?'

'And then what?'

'Pippa…'

'What if we don't work out?'

'I'm asking you for a holiday, Pippa, not a lifetime commitment!'

'I know that,' she snapped. 'I told you at the start that I'm not brilliant at long-term relationships.'

'It's just a couple of weeks in Scotland,' he pointed out.

'For you, maybe!' Her chair scraped as she pushed it back. 'I'm going to do the meds.'

Luke's mood wasn't great as he headed for the on-call rooms.

He knew he was changing the rules by suggesting a holiday, but he was changing too. He wanted more—and that was new to him. Usually he was more than ready to walk away.

Not now.

But what did he have to complain about? Luke thought, when he saw Evan sitting in the near-empty canteen.

And, yes, he was changing—because rather than walking on by he took a breath and forced himself to walk in.

'Hey.' Luke went over to Evan. 'Taking a break?'

'Yes, I'm just…' Evan stared at his uneaten roll. 'I don't know if we should show Darcy the recording of the funeral service or talk to him about it…'

Where was Pippa when he needed her? Luke thought. He'd been hoping to offer his polite condolences, even answer some medical questions, but this was much harder.

'I don't doubt you'll make the right choices with Darcy,' he said.

Evan nodded wearily, but then a look of agony flashed across his features, so acute that he might just as well have been punched, and as he folded over, Luke was certain he was reliving his choices that fatal morning.

Luke knew he was a good surgeon, but in this department he didn't exactly excel. Then he thought again of Pippa…how her words had brought comfort that night when he'd been berating himself for not transferring Hamish to be with his twin.

'Evan,' he said, placing his hand on the man's shoulder. 'I know you're questioning your decision not to leave the twins at home that morning.' He felt the man's grief beneath his fingers. 'But I've seen the consequences of that far too many times.'

Evan wept.

'I have,' Luke said. 'I've had to sit with parents who *have* made the wrong choices on many occasions. And I am telling you now, you did the right thing.'

'Thank you,' Evan said.

But Luke wasn't finished. 'May I say…?' He took a breath. 'May I say that I'm in awe of the two of you and how you've handled things with Darcy.'

He carried on comforting Evan as best he could. And afterwards, instead of heading to the on-call rooms, he went back up to Paediatrics.

To see Pippa again?

He didn't know why.

To say what?

He wasn't sure of that either.

He just knew that he could not leave things as they were.

He was used to dealing with the usual sulks after a break-up, but he'd asked her to join him in Scotland and he couldn't make sense of her reaction. He was still trying to keep things light—he'd told her he wasn't proposing marriage!

Then he stilled.

There she was, sitting at the desk with the lamp on. She was wearing a cardigan to keep out the chill, and he realised that her contact lenses must have been irritating her eyes because she was wearing glasses.

Suddenly, he was transported back to a day many years ago…

Philippa.

Who'd liked French and Art and…

It was coming back to him now.

Cake.

Philippa—which it turned out she didn't like to be called…

Julia's sister Philippa.

And now he knew her better, he could guess why she hadn't revealed the connection that day.

He watched her reach for a box of tissues and blow her nose. He wasn't vain enough to think it was to do with his leaving.

But he was sure enough in himself to know that it played a part.

A bigger part than he'd ever considered…?

Was Pippa actually…in love with him? And if she was, how the hell did he feel about that?

'Hey,' Luke said, walking over, and she blinked and looked up. 'You do have a super-memory.'

'Do I?'

He nodded. 'It *was* me in the library.'

'Told you.' She smiled.

'You were right—I had been crying that day.'

'So you do remember?'

'I'd just gone home to get my swim kit and caught my father cheating.' He gave a grim smile and then came around and took a seat beside her. 'I insisted that he tell my mother. I thought I was doing the right thing…'

Pippa looked at him.

'She didn't take it well, to say the least.' He exhaled sharply. 'She had a breakdown and ended up in hospital for a few weeks. I thought I'd killed her.'

'I'm so sorry,' Pippa said. 'No wonder you messed up your chemistry exam.'

'Bloody fragmentation.' He rolled his eyes. 'That's why I stay out of people's personal lives,' he said. 'Why I don't do long term…' His eyes never left her face. 'What about you?'

'Oh, I'd love to do long term,' Pippa readily admitted, but then hastily retracted. 'Maybe someday.'

'Yeah…'

'Thanks for remembering,' she said. 'It's silly, really, but it meant a lot to me at the time. I hated it that you'd—' Pippa pressed her lips together.

'Forgotten?'

She nodded. 'It doesn't matter now.'

They stopped talking as Evan came onto the ward and asked about Amber.

'She's asleep,' Pippa told him. 'Do you want me to show you where she is?'

'Let her sleep,' Evan said. 'I might go and lie down with Darcy.'

'So,' Luke said, when they were alone again, 'am I booking the French restaurant? I'll be barred if I cancel on them twice…'

'I don't think so.' She shook her head. 'No.'

Luke checked no one was around and leant in. 'You don't want champagne and a lot of sex?' he asked, feeling the heat from her burning cheeks. 'One more wild night…?'

'I'd rather give it a miss, thanks.'

He was dismayed, but he noticed what it cost her to force out a smile.

Liar!

He didn't say that, though.

As he walked across the ward, he glanced through the glass and saw Evan giving Darcy a drink with a straw and pulling a funny face to make his son laugh.

His own father had done that for him when he'd had his tonsils out. He'd come down from Theatre to check on him in the night, and persuaded him to take some fluids.

Luke didn't care that it was three a.m. He fired his father a quick text before he could change his mind.

Do you want to meet for lunch?

Matthew Harris didn't seem to care about the late hour either. Perhaps he was on a night shift himself.

Does midday work?

It did.

Luke looked back at Pip, who was carrying an angry toddler, bringing him to sit with her at the desk.

Pippa, he amended.

Yet he saw Philippa.

And he actually ached for all she'd been through.

She hadn't just been forgotten by her parents.

She had never really been loved.

Julia wasn't the ghost in that family. Pippa was.

Then, hearing a tap on the window, he turned and saw Darcy in his father's arms, smiling.

For the sake of his son, Evan was too.

As Darcy waved though the glass, so too did Evan, and of course Luke waved back, then gave a little thumbs-up to Evan.

What a brave man, Luke thought, and he realised that the Williams family were going to make it.

Despite all that life had thrown at them, they would get through this.

In their own way…

CHAPTER FIFTEEN

Pippa woke at two in the afternoon, completely at sixes and sevens.

She wanted to see Luke, of course she did, but she honestly didn't know if she could get through a romantic dinner without falling apart at the seams.

Let alone sex.

And yet she wanted him so badly.

Luke's re-entry into her life had indeed muddied the waters, and there wasn't a soul she could discuss it with.

Well, maybe one soul…

Pippa had never really found any comfort from going to the cemetery.

Julia's was possibly the best-kept grave in the place, given that her mother was here most days.

Today, though, Pippa had it to herself. She took off her coat and placed it on the ground then sat on it. Staring at the grave she looked at all the little things her mother brought and frequently re-arranged.

'I wish I could talk to you,' Pippa said suddenly, her own voice surprising her. 'We always could talk.'

It was true.

She and Julia had tried not to upset her mother, but they had been more honest when it was just the two of them.

'Luke's been working at The Primary,' Pippa said, and realised that on top of everything else she felt guilty. As if she were stepping into her sister's life or her dreams—except that Julia and Luke had never really existed. 'We've been seeing each other. Just a casual thing,' she added hastily. But there was no reason to lie. 'Well, according to Luke... He's asked me to visit him when he moves Scotland, but there's no point.' She voiced another thing that scared her too. 'Can you imagine Mum's face if I told her?'

But in the past trying to protect her mother hadn't solved anything. Pushing down her feelings...even the fact of her existence...

'Pippa!'

She turned at the sound of her mother's voice, and saw that she carried the gardening basket that she always brought to the cemetery.

'I wasn't expecting to see you here!'

'Hi, Mum.' Pippa stood to give her mother a kiss, but it was a haphazard one as she was pulling on her gardening gloves at the same time. Then she put a little mat onto the frosty grass to kneel upon. 'I just thought I'd come... Have a few moments...' Pippa said falteringly.

'That's nice.'

'I was just telling Julia...' she took a breath '... that Luke Harris has been working at The Primary for the past month.'

'Oh!'

That had got her mother's attention.

'We've been seeing each other...'

'Pippa!' Her mother's eyes darted to the grave. 'Not here.'

'Then where?' Pippa said. 'Julia can't hear, Mum, and if she can, well...' She took a deep breath. 'If she can hear then it's nice for me to have someone I can actually talk to about myself...about how *I'm* feeling...'

Her mother stood up and pulled off her gloves. 'The one little relationship Julia had!' she hissed. 'Of all the men in the world, you have to take the one that she cared for the most.'

'Of all the men in the world,' Pippa shouted, 'he was the one *I* cared for the most!'

She took a shuddering breath and felt the sting of tears as she admitted out loud the truth she'd been fighting not to reveal, even to herself.

'He was the one. Even back then.'

She stormed off.

'Pippa!' her mother called out.

'What?' Pippa turned around but did not retrace a single step. 'What do you want?'

'I had no idea about—'

'How could you have? The only thing we ever talk about is Julia! It was my birthday last week. My thirtieth!'

'I know that. There's a card and—'

'I don't *want* a card!' Pippa was too upset to even shout any more. 'Or money. I wanted you to remember...to make a fuss. Just for once not to make me feel guilty for existing.'

'Pippa!'

'You don't have room for me in your heart.'

She felt tears splashing down her cheeks, and she didn't know if she was crying for Julia, for her lost relationship with her mother, or even for Luke, who surely didn't want her desperate love either.

'It's true…'

'Pippa!' Her mother's voice was shocked. 'I did my best…'

'Well, it wasn't enough.'

She practically ran from the cemetery, gulping back sobs as she hurried into the Underground, desperate to make it home…

And there she cried like she never had before.

She had hidden her tears from Julia, and later from her parents, and in the end from herself too. Now Pippa curled up on the bed and cried, and it sounded so much like Amber sobbing her heart out that at the thought of that little family Pippa only wept harder.

It didn't help, though. Because she wanted Luke's arms to be holding her. She wanted the one thing he would never give, and she couldn't put herself through this any longer.

Yes, Julia had been able to laugh and squeeze every ounce out of her life, but she wasn't here any more. Her advice had run out.

Pippa really was alone.

She gulped as she admitted the truth to herself: she was scared.

Scared of being in love.

Scared of being left behind.

Scared of being forgotten.

As Pippa's sobbing slowed, it felt to her as if her sister was in the room. It truly felt as if she could hear Julia's breathless voice…as if Julia was stroking her hair.

'Pip, everybody gets scared at times. I just tell myself I'll let myself be scared tomorrow…'

It had made little sense at the time, but it made every sense now!

Before she could change her mind, Pippa called for a taxi. She had precisely fifteen minutes to transform her red and swollen face into something French-restaurant-worthy.

She slicked on some lipstick and hoped her wild hair would cover the worst as she pulled on the lilac dress he'd stood her up in once already.

Then she pulled on heels and took the Santorini picture from the ledge.

She was ready.

Ready for one final night with Luke.

Then she'd tell him what he could do with his emotionally uninvolved relationships and walk out of his life.

Whatever the day brought—or the night—Pippa vowed to deal with it by telling herself she could be scared tomorrow. Just like Julia.

It only dawned on her as she buzzed his intercom that she'd told him not to book the restaurant.

'Pippa!'

He buzzed her up and stood at the door, wearing

the bottom half of a suit, naked from the hips up and holding a glass of wine. She could hear music in the background.

'I thought you weren't…'

'I'm intruding,' Pippa said, suddenly worried that her replacement was already in situ! 'I should have called first.'

'Of course not.' He held the door open. 'What's this?'

'The Santorini picture you liked.' She gave him a wicked smile. 'It might help clinch the sale.'

'Or have the buyers running for the door. Are you okay?' he checked.

Perhaps he'd noticed that she looked a bit off.

'Contact lenses!' Pippa said. 'Allergies.'

'Goodness,' he replied, and poured her a glass of red. 'You're not allergic to this, I hope?'

'No, that would be lovely.' She took a rather hefty gulp. 'I had a row with my mum,' she admitted.

'Bad?' he asked.

They certainly weren't playing traffic controllers tonight, because she didn't put her hand up to halt him. 'Dreadful. I think I said too much.'

'Well, I can't really imagine you doing that,' Luke admitted, 'but even if you did, there's a lot of hurt and trauma there. Some things have to be said.'

'Yes.'

'If it makes you feel better, I had a row with my dad,' he told her. 'I took your advice and went for lunch with him.' Luke sighed. 'We started arguing in the car park, before we'd even gone in.'

'Oh!'

'But then we actually managed to eat lunch. I don't understand the details, and frankly I don't want to.' He rolled his eyes. 'We've called a truce.'

'That's so good.'

'Thanks to you,' he said. 'Look, I wouldn't want their marriage—but then I don't have to live it, do I?'

'No.'

'Oh, and I told him I'm getting them tickets for that interactive theatre thing for Christmas and that he's to take my mother this time.'

Pippa laughed, and it was a real laugh. Because that was what he did, even on dark days: he made her smile. No, she would never regret this crazy month.

'Is it too late to book the restaurant?'

'Sorry.' He shook his head. 'Not a hope on a Saturday night.'

'Oh, well,' Pippa said. 'Just sex, then...'

'Wow!' he said, blinking.

'Look, I know I've been a bit difficult. But I did warn you I was lousy at relationships.'

'You're hard work for a fling.'

'Yes.'

'But more than worth it.' He placed down his glass and then took hers too and pulled her into his arms. 'How did you leave things with your mum?' he asked.

'I don't know,' Pippa admitted, feeling his naked chest against her cheek and allowing herself the bliss of being held in his arms. 'I can smell baby powder...'

'I like it,' he said. 'I bought a can of my own...'

'You didn't!' she said.

'No, I pinched one of yours for work.' He lifted her face and gave her a soft kiss. 'I'm so glad you came.'

How close she'd come to missing this... Pippa didn't even want to consider it. She could lose herself in his kiss for ever, and she loved the easy way he dealt with her dress, lifting her arms and pulling it over her head.

Taking her hand, he led her to the bedroom. 'Excuse the mess.'

She didn't care if the bed was unmade, especially when he was pushing her down onto it. She let go as he slid her knickers off and delivered the bliss that only he could with his mouth.

'Sorry, Pip,' he said, just as she was about to come. He left her on the edge of heaven as he unzipped and then, patient and tender no more, he was inside her. 'I couldn't wait.'

She wrapped her thighs around him and clung on, because, in truth, neither could she. A rollercoaster called Luke had thundered back into her life, and now he was looking right at her as he took her, and she was looking back at him.

Until she couldn't any more. And then she closed her eyes to the bliss and the noise of them coming together.

'Damn, Pip,' he said as he lay on top of her. 'You've messed up my plans…'

It had been the most rapid, intense sex of her life. She resurfaced, a little bewildered, not just by his words but because all the familiar landmarks were missing.

No cushions.

No rugs.

No ugly pictures on the walls.

'That was unexpected!' he said, as she lay staring at the ceiling. 'I hope the estate agent doesn't bring someone to view—'

'Stop!' She was startled by the horror of that thought. 'I thought it was under offer?'

'Not any more.'

'Did they withdraw?'

'Please don't talk about withdrawing,' he said, and with his hand sliding between her thighs it was indecent with meaning.

'I told you. I'm on the Pill. I take it religiously. I've got the—' She took a breath and then just said it. 'I'm a carrier.'

'Well, thankfully I'm not.'

She frowned. 'How do you know?'

'I got a test. That's what I was trying to discuss.'

'Why would you go and get tested?'

'Because I felt bad for being careless that morning, and I guessed there was a reasonable chance you had the gene. If there were consequences… Well, that would have been one thing we'd have needed to know.'

'You went and had a test?' Her voice was incredulous. 'You did that?'

'I was hardly strapped to monitors and asked to run for an hour with a mask on. It was a cheek swab.'

'But…why?'

'Because I care about you, Pippa. Because we'd have needed to know….'

He said it so calmly, and in such a matter-of-fact voice, when all she'd ever known was panic and fear around the subject.

'Come on—get dressed. We need to eat. Chicken Provençal is waiting.'

'But you couldn't get a reservation.'

'No, but I could get them to deliver. I just need to warm it. We're not eating dinner naked.'

'Why not?'

'I have standards.'

He pulled a shirt out of its plastic bag and retrieved the bottom half of his suit from the floor, then went to select a tie.

'Are we seriously dressing up?'

'Yes,' Luke said. 'We're celebrating.'

Remembering her vow to face anything now and be scared tomorrow, Pippa retrieved the clothes she'd so hurriedly taken off and went into his bathroom.

He'd spun her completely!

But she was going to be brave and fearless…

'Dinner!' he called.

She walked into the living room and found that

he'd set the table. There was even a candle stuck in a wine bottle.

'This looks incredible,' Pippa said as he brought over two plates.

'Never tell Anton that I microwaved it,' Luke said, laughing, and he let her take a gorgeous herby mouthful. 'Or that we had red wine with it...'

'I won't,' Pippa said, and didn't add that she'd never get the chance to now. She was through with sniping and being insecure. Instead, she would enjoy the gorgeous food and wine, and of course the company too.

'Pip...' Luke said, and she looked up at his serious tone. 'I haven't been completely honest...'

'That's okay,' Pippa said.

After all, she hadn't been completely honest with him either. He'd have run a mile, Pippa knew, if he'd known the strength of her feelings for him.

'The thing is,' Luke said, 'I need a break...'

'I get it,' Pippa said. 'This has been great. It really has—'

'Pip!' he interrupted. 'I mean from work.'

'Oh.'

'I'm not going to Scotland for work,' he told her. 'I had a great mentor in Philadelphia, and he was very insistent that it's important to take a break and get away every so often. He goes fishing...'

'You're going fishing?'

'No.'

He was very serious, Pippa realised, and she put down her cutlery.

'I need a month or two away from broken bodies,' he said. 'I scoffed at Carl at the time, but I can see now he was right. I love my job, and I'm going to keep doing it, but I'm going to make sure I take my breaks more seriously.'

'And not take on a month's casual work while you sell your flat?' Pippa said, and raised her glass. 'I'll drink to that!'

'Come with me,' Luke said. 'I know the off-duty's tricky, and that you may have a new job soon, but…'

Pippa was determined to be the bravest she'd ever been. And instead of declining, instead of running from potential hurt, she followed her heart and nodded. 'I'd love to come to Scotland.'

'You're sure?'

'Very.' She gave her bravest smile. 'Can't leave you sex-starved in your little stone cottage.'

'I'll get dessert,' he said, and looked at her. 'What are you smiling at?'

'You,' Pippa admitted. 'How you can just end a conversation—an important one—as if you're calling for the bill!' She even laughed. 'Will you wave me off in the morning?'

'I hope not,' Luke responded, and disappeared into the kitchen.

He came out with a cake, lit with one long, slender candle.

'You didn't have to do that…' She laughed, but there was a lump in her throat that he was trying to make that awful birthday up to her. 'I told you, it was no big deal…'

'It's a very big deal,' Luke said. 'Because as well as asking you to join me in Scotland, I *would* like a lifetime commitment.'

He put down the cake.

And it was not just any cake!

'You deserve cake on your birthday. I'm so sorry I added to the misery of this year's. Now, I was going to make one myself, but in the end I left it to the experts,' Luke explained to his stunned audience. 'Smoked almond praline and chocolate.'

But Pippa wasn't interested in the ingredients, no matter how delicious they sounded. Neither was she interested in the pale white candle, with its twitching flame. She was only interested in the appalling piping that looked so at odds with the exquisite, delicate cake…

Surely they'd delivered the wrong cake. Because instead of *Happy Birthday* it read: *Marry me.*

'I decided not to attempt a question mark,' Luke joked. 'There wasn't room.'

'I thought they'd delivered the wrong cake…'

'It's the right cake. Well, it's certainly the one I piped.'

'*You* piped this?'

'Much to Anton's scorn.'

'Why?'

'It's the little things,' he said, as she had to him one day. 'Though, before you say yes or no, in the interests of full disclosure…'

'You have an ex-wife?' Pippa checked, and he shook his head.

'Children?'

'Close,' Luke said. 'A puppy with bathroom issues.'

'You're taking Sausage?'

He rolled his eyes as he nodded. 'I have to walk him in an hour and then drag all his stuff over here. Oh, and I've taken the flat off the market.'

'Why?'

'I want your dark art on my walls.' He took her hands. 'I don't want to a be a lone wolf. I don't want my parents' messes and mistakes to serve as my lessons in life. I love you, and I think you might have a little more than just a crush on me…'

He knew! Pippa realised.

But he couldn't know just how deeply she loved him.

'I love you too much,' Pippa admitted, and then she looked over to him, wanting to make sure he knew how big her love was. 'I made a heart in art after the library that day. I painted it Kobicha-brown with russet and copper flecks. It was the closest I could get to the colour of your eyes.'

'Gosh…' He pondered that for a moment. 'Have you still got it?'

'Yes…' There was more. 'And I fantasised about you a few times…'

'That's fine.'

'No…' She flushed with guilt. 'I mean, when I was with someone else…'

'Well, I'm glad I could help!' He laughed.

'Luke, I love you, and I think I always have.'

'And I want your love. I want you to hole up with me in Scotland. If you can get time off, that is. And I'll talk to your parents.'

'Let me,' Pippa said. 'Luke, you're still on their mantelpiece. A picture of you and Julia.'

'I understand.' He nodded thoughtfully, then said, 'I don't particularly want our parents at our wedding…'

He held her hands, but it wasn't enough contact so she came around the table and sat on his knee.

'Look, I get that it might not work for you. They've only got one child. So if you think we ought to—'

'Just us,' she said.

'Just us?' Luke repeated. 'Is that a yes?'

'You didn't need the question mark, Luke.'

He'd had her heart since she was sixteen years old.

'It's always been a yes.'

CHAPTER SIXTEEN

IN FEBRUARY SHE would be starting her new role at The Primary, and Luke had landed a plum consultancy job at a famous teaching hospital—one without the shadow of his father hanging over it.

'Six consecutive weeks off each year...'

It was written into his contract, and even though Pippa didn't have quite enough pull to get it written into hers, she had told Miss Brett that she'd be taking the same.

As for Pippa's parents...she'd told them that she was serious about Luke.

At least they were talking...

And the picture on the mantelpiece had thankfully been taken down.

But right now, it was their wedding day.

Pippa wasn't even nervous. How could she be when she felt as if this day had been etched into her lifeline—as if they'd been destined for each other and finally the world had caught up with what had been written in the stars.

As well as that, she was grappling with new underwear, as Luke watched on.

'We're not having sex again until we're legal,' he told her.

'Then hurry up and make me your wife!' Pippa laughed as she pulled on a gorgeous jade dress. 'My favourite colour...'

She looked down at her stunning engagement ring, which sported an emerald with every shade of captivating green—even army-green. She loved it so much.

'Here,' he said, handing her a small box. 'Your flowers.'

Heather and thistles.

Spiky and soft.

A lot like life.

And—also a lot like life—very beautiful too.

Luke picked up Sausage, who was dressed in a tartan bow for the occasion, and they headed off to be wed.

The Wee Neuk was the smallest wedding venue in Edinburgh's City Chambers, and for Pippa and Luke it was the perfect venue for such a special day.

The celebrant greeted them warmly, along with their two witnesses. Their hands were wrapped in silk rope, and they exchanged the traditional hand-fasting vows they had chosen.

'Do you, Luke, take Philippa to be your wife? To be her constant friend, her partner in life, and her true love? To love her without reservation, honour and respect her, protect her from harm, comfort her in times of distress, and to grow with her in mind and spirit?'

'I do,' Luke said in a confident, clear voice.

And those vows, those words, meant everything to Pippa. She took a breath, and the celebrant asked her the same questions.

'Do you, Philippa, take Luke to be your husband? To be his constant friend…?'

Till then, Pippa had done all she could to hold it together. She'd never thought it would be Luke's eyes that would fill with tears.

Of course she knew that he loved her, but it was then, in that moment, that she understood just how much, and what these words meant to him.

'…and to grow with him in mind and spirt?' the celebrant asked.

'I do,' Pippa said, and then she looked at the man her heart loved, and reiterated, 'I really do.'

And with the rope removed, and their promises still hanging in the air, he pulled her into his arms and held her.

Pippa felt a moment of bewilderment and wonder. 'We're family now.'

'We are,' Luke agreed. He looked at the white-gold ring she'd placed on his finger, and then back to her, and said, 'You've got me now.'

And it wasn't said in an arrogant way. He wasn't teasing her for her devotion. He was gently addressing the fact that she'd never really been loved. Well, apart from by one other person…

'Are you ready?' he asked, when the paperwork was all done.

Because there was one more place they needed to be before they headed to a beautiful hotel for the first night of their honeymoon.

And then off to Skye…

Luke held her hand as a driver took them on the hour and a half journey to St Andrew's. There was a light snowfall, and Pippa looked out at the North Sea, which was churning and grey, and then to the gorgeous buildings dusted in white. She gasped at the splendour of the university.

'They won't mind?' she checked.

'I told you—I've made all the arrangements.'

As she stepped out of the car a piper was playing—by chance, Pippa thought at first. But then he walked ahead of them, leading them to the chapel.

'Amazing Grace' had been played at her sister's funeral, but it sounded so much sweeter now, and this time around she was free to cry, even on this, the happiest day of her life.

'I came,' Pippa said, recalling one of her conversations with Julia, when her sister had asked her to visit St Andrew's in her place. 'Thank you,' she said.

And she laid her little posy on the steps, because without her sister's brave spirit spurring her on she might never have had the courage to risk her heart and say yes to Luke's proposition. Even if they had only lasted a month, Pippa knew it would still have been worth it.

'I love you, Julia.'

She always had and always would.

Then she turned to Luke, who was holding Sausage, and took his hand as they walked back to the car. 'I wish she'd been here today.'

'You'd have been fighting like two cats over me…' he teased.

'Stop it!' She nudged him playfully, and then, in the midst of her tears, she started to laugh. And it was so nice to actually laugh as she spoke about her sister. 'You're so sure of yourself!'

'Oh, I am today,' he said.

So sure of their love.

* * * * *